Flying to Nowhere

'Very exciting... most beaut
chosen as the words of a pc

"The shape-shifting nature of its plot, and a precision of language
which serves to enhance its mystery, are the chief pleasures of
Flying to Nowhere" – Adam-Mars Jones, *Sunday Times*

"A masterly performance... a significant fictional debut"
– *Glasgow Herald*

The Adventures of Speedfall

"A dazzling new farce—a sort of *Yes, Principal* version of the
academic corridors of power..." – Gillian Greenwood, *The
Literary Review*

"At last the real thing" – Nicholas Best, *Financial Times*

"This is an elegantly written and frequent hilarious collection"
– *Sunday Times*

"Donnish humour at its most urbane, ingenious and eccentric"
– John Mellors, *The Spectator*

Tell It Me Again

"An abiding pleasure" – *Evening Standard*

The Burning Boys

"A striking and clever short novel about a boy growing up, set in
the Forties, but with insights that are not dated" – Philip
Howard, Novel of the Week, *Observer*

"Superb... a novel of special quality" – *Evening Standard*

"Here is a short book whose size is not tailored with an eye to fashion but with a sure sense of what is artistically right. Wherever you cut it, the aces are high, the story rich" – Candia McWilliam, *Guardian*

Look Twice

"Sheer fun… it is indeed enormously and intelligently entertaining; its pace and flair is such that it would make a breathtaking, if prohibitively expensive, film" – Nick Hornby, *Sunday Times*

"It's funny, it's clever and it is great great fun" – *Evening Standard*

"Tantalising and amusing" – *Sunday Telegraph*

The Worm and the Star

"*The Worm and the Star* is a lesson in structure to novelists, a lesson in clarity to poets, and, to readers, a deeply civilised and civilising gift" – Glyn Maxwell, *Guardian*

A Skin Diary

"Superb" – *Times Literary Supplement*

"In part the novel is about language itself and sees Fuller, who has written more than 30 books of poetry and prose, in full flight" – Russell Celyn Jones, *Times*

"Rich and marvellous writing indeed" – James Jauncey, *The Scotsman*

"Fuller's imagistic flair and delight in language conjure an elemental magic" – Jason Thompson, *Harpers & Queen*

The Memoirs of Laetitia Horsepole

"This is an extraordinarily good novel. Deftly clever and full of fun. [It] tells us more about being female and smart in Georgian England than a whole slew of social history books ever could" – Kathryn Hughes, *Daily Telegraph*

"Fuller combines intelligence and ravishing lyricism with a gorgeous gift for storytelling… Fuller is something special. Those who want to give their reading clubs something pleasurable to tackle should put their hands up for Laetitia. She won't let them down" – *Literary Review*

Flawed Angel

"*Flawed Angel* is a philosophical tale in the style of *Rasselas*, and Fuller devises, with great ingenuity, a society that has tried to provide civilised solutions to eternal problems" – A. S. Byatt, *Guardian*

"A repertory of wonders… this fairy tale will surely outlive him" – *The Times*

"Sumptuously written… a curiously beautiful and life-affirming story" – *Telegraph*

"A delicious treat" – *Guardian*

"A novel as intellectually provocative as it is emotionally beguiling" – Lucy Powell, *Observer*

LOSER

LOSER

JOHN FULLER

Shoestring Press

All rights reserved. No part of this work covered by the copyright herein may be reproduced or used in any means—graphic, electronic, or mechanical, including copying, recording, taping, or information storage and retrieval systems—without written permission of the publisher.

Printed by imprintdigital
Upton Pyne, Exeter
www.digital.imprint.co.uk

Typesetting and cover design by The Book Typesetters
us@thebooktypesetters.com
07422 598 168
www.thebooktypesetters.com

Published by Shoestring Press
19 Devonshire Avenue, Beeston, Nottingham, NG9 1BS
0115 925 1827
www.shoestringpress.co.uk

First published 2021
© Copyright: John Fuller
© Cover photo: 'Galaxy in Yosemite' by Anson Yang (Unsplash.com)

The moral right of the author has been asserted.

ISBN 978-1-912524-74-7

1.

Graham Horrocks was used to hearing voices beyond his hedge, but this was different. Not the aimless dialogue of a strolling family trying to reach the river, or the irritating sounds of children, but something like an argument.

A man's voice was saying No.

"Nah…", it whined, over and over.

A woman's voice persisted beneath it, but he couldn't hear what she said. She sounded insistent about something, going on and on.

"Nah…", said the other voice, indistinctly and complainingly (or was it just "Ah…"?).

The woman was being reasonable, as if quietly making out a case, and the man was objecting. Or it might have been her name, because his voice occasionally rose as if he were addressing her.

The voices didn't move away. Their owners weren't going anywhere.

Graham was put out by their presence, too far away to be heard properly, too near not to be intrusive. He had gone down to the pod at the end of the garden with the intention of at last making some sort of a real start in sorting out Maddie's things. He had looked around, and moved some pencils from one shelf to another, and picked up a music stand that had tipped over. But then, as on several earlier occasions, he had simply stood in the middle of the pod and induced himself to weep. He didn't fully cry, but stood there clenching and unclenching his fingers with a tragic rictus on his face which he could see in his mind's eye, and felt to be appropriate to his feelings.

"The poor widower," he thought, "reduced to indecision."

He tried to summon up the sound of Maddie's cello behind his screwed-up eyes, accompanied by the rhythmical nod of her head and occasional tossing back of her hair, but the sense of his own abandonment seemed to get in the way. She was gone, and now was of course nowhere, but he was still here, and so long as he suffered he knew that he still existed. Sometimes that knowledge was sufficient. After all, what else was there to be done?

He could hear nothing of the outside world in the pod, since it was elaborately sound-proofed. In fact, it had been constructed to the highest sound-proofing specifications, with multi-layered insulation of rubber strips, dense acoustic boards, membranes and claddings. Before Maddie had bought it, she had been very aware that her practising might have been disturbing the Peacocks and the Sherwoods, their immediate neighbours, or anyone in the Close for that matter. Besides, she always said that she needed a bolt-hole. The house was far too small. Graham had laughed with disbelief at that. They had four bedrooms! But at the same time, he felt a pang of shame that he might never have properly provided for a woman who had been brought up at Trace Priory in Gloucestershire and whose father had been a Brigadier-General. They should have been living on Boar's Hill, and not in an inter-war cul-de-sac in North Oxford whose only redeeming feature was its concealed access to the River Cherwell. Maddie had, however, lived her life with him in remarkable dignity and tolerance, and had (as the generous obituary in the *Oxford Times* stressed) "contributed significantly to the musical life of the city." That, he thought proudly, had surely justified her spending over £40K of what was, after all, her own, or at least the Brigadier-General's, money on 25 square metres of oak-clad pod in the bottom of their garden in Yarnfield Close, from which none of her savage arpeggios could be heard.

2

Stepping outside it now, having made no inroads at all on the piles of personal and musical life that Maddie had left behind, he was immediately irritated to hear the voices continuing their altercation, the drone of the woman and the occasional whine of the man. Why were they just there, and not moving on? At times like this he deserved some peace.

The lane that ran parallel to the river was the distance of a field from it, so that the pole of an occasionally adventurous punt looked only like a small exclamation mark between the willows. To get to the lane you had to find the narrow alley at the end of the Close between Ann Sims's house and the Peacocks'. Not many people did, of course, since it was off the beaten track of tourists. Sometimes a punt-load of students might come the other way, already tipsy and on the look-out for the Hanover Arms, and turning back in disappointment at finding themselves nowhere near it in what felt like a desolate suburb. But mostly it was used by local residents to exercise their dogs or to pick blackberries, and there were some dens made by children. It wasn't the place for an argument still going on after ten minutes.

Graham walked back up to the house, resenting the voices as though they were intruders and somehow responsible for his failure to cope with his renewed grief. He could have opened the old overgrown gate at the bottom of his garden that led to the lane where the two were arguing, and gone out to see what sort of objectionable people they were, to stare at them perhaps, until they became uncomfortable and went away. Yes, he could have done that. He thought of the bitter rebukes he might have made, as a righteous and disturbed householder. But he didn't have the courage to do so.

Father Eustace was content to follow his Labrador, Effie, wherever she chose to go because he knew her habits well and she would always come back to him in response to his short whistle, to nudge his knees and look up at him expectantly for a communication of some kind.

Sometimes he walked with her to Crossland Road and around a couple of blocks of broad pavement, where she had fun sniffing the passage of earlier dogs, but he was wary of the traffic. Cars looking in vain for parking places became impatient and unreliable. He preferred taking her down the Yarnfield Close alley and into the fields by the river. There she was perfectly safe, and much happier.

He left his own house, no. 10, passed nos. 9 and 8, gently caressing the fuchsia that hung over the wall of no. 8, and eventually turned right again into the alley. The alley was bordered by a high fence over which hung on the right the Leylandii of Mrs Sims of no. 6 and on the left the plum trees of the Peacocks at no. 5. Its entrance wasn't obvious, since it was overhung with foliage and the pavement in front of it was unbroken, sweeping round in the curve of the turning circle that concluded the brief length of Yarnfield Close. A perfect disguise: any stranger venturing into the Close would be confronted with the appearance of quiet conclusion and domesticity. Bill Peacock might be washing his car. A cul-de-sac, obviously.

At the end of the alley Father Eustace turned left where the overgrown lane headed vaguely northwards. Effie had already done so, and had found something to interest her in the base of the bay tree that over the years had grown beneath and through the Peacocks' back fence.

"What have you got there, old girl?" said Father Eustace, taking his dog by the collar and detaching some plastic from her jaws. It was a sandwich container, with some remains of crust and filling inside.

"No, I don't think that's for you," he said. "Wouldn't agree with you at all."

He held it out between his finger and thumb, wondering where he might get rid of it.

Graham Horrocks of no. 4 was coming towards him along the lane. Effie forgot about the sandwich container and bounded to meet him. Graham stopped in his tracks, lifting his arms slightly so that his hands might be out of reach of the dog's tongue.

Effie was fascinated by Graham, more than any of her master's neighbours that she was likely to encounter on her exciting walks.

4

What was it? It was his smell. Nobody is prepared to admit that they smell, but a dog will be aware of it, nosing about in a seated guest's trouser-fly or snuffling his shoes, and it is likely to be embarrassing. Graham's smell was different, an aura that belonged to no specific part of his person. Much of it was a sweet earthy manifestation of singed leaves that Effie connected with compost heaps and the rare blissful site of an illegal bonfire. It was, to any human being who detected it, the sign of a moral and social failing: Graham had refused to give up smoking, thinking that the medical horrors now obligatory on cigarette packets were a gross example of the creeping nanny state. But to Effie it was a divine vegetal emanation that connected him to the soil and to the ordure she loved. She wagged her tail, and looked at him eagerly for a sign of blessing. The blessing of the god of tobacco.

"Effie, come here!" commanded Father Eustace. He knew that Graham didn't get on with his dog. Effie briefly looked up at Graham as if for confirmation, panting genially, and then returned to her master.

"Nice day, Graham," said Father Eustace in greeting, holding Effie's collar.

"The day is nice enough," replied Graham. "But this isn't very nice."

He also was holding something in his hand. As he came closer, Father Eustace saw that it was a syringe.

"Dear me," he said. "That's not good at all."

"No," said Graham. "And I heard some very unsavoury characters in the lane yesterday. They were arguing about something."

"Did you see who they were?"

"No, but they sounded young. Druggies, I should think."

Graham looked about him pleasantly as he said this, giving surreptitious glances here and there as though seeking approval from invisible bystanders. His little smile seemed designed to bestow his own approval on himself in case none were forthcoming from Father Eustace, who was often slow to commit himself in conversation.

"Do you think they were dealing, then?"

"No idea. What's that you've found there?"

Father Eustace held out the sandwich container. He laughed.

"More unwanted waste. The consumer society."

Graham pulled a face.

"But this is actually illegal." He indicated the needle.

"Not very clever, is it?" agreed Father Eustace.

They stood there, each with his disgusting trophy. Neither of them was particularly eager to get away, so they began to discuss the consumer society and what it might mean to want not to belong to it. Graham remembered the hippy communes of the Californian deserts and how they were only possible if the hippies were able to pick up discarded chairs and fridges for free from the pavements of affluent neighbourhoods, probably where their own parents were living. Father Eustace nodded, but out of discretion didn't mention the counter-arguments that, perhaps irrationally, occurred to him: the miraculous loaves and fishes, and the saintly disciplines of the Desert Fathers. His mind was rather inclined to go off at tangents.

"That sandwich," said Graham, "was probably stolen from the bins of past-the-sell-by stuff outside Marks and Spencer."

"Quite so," said Father Eustace, again not admitting that his church negotiated gifts of food from local supermarkets and distributed it in hostels for the homeless. "But perhaps needs-must?"

This was as far as he would go in discussion with a man he knew to be intolerant. But he also knew that part of his vocation was appeasement.

"Nobody needs to inject themselves with dangerous substances," said Graham, "and then leave the needles around for children to find. Or dogs."

He looked at Effie without the remotest appearance of concern for her well being.

"Why should they do it in public places," he added. "Why don't they do it at home?"

Father Eustace was drawn by this.

"Quite possibly they have no home," he said.

"Turned out by their parents for being druggies, no doubt."

"Ah, well," said Father Eustace uneasily. "I think the problem may go a little deeper than that."

"It's a problem all right," said Graham robustly. "They're everywhere these days. Sleeping in doorways, and begging. It's terrible in Oxford."

"Oxford's always been a meeting-place for travellers," said Father Eustace. "It's right in the centre of the country, a kind of cross-roads if you like."

"Oh, you mean *tramps*," said Graham brightly, emphasising the word as though they were now talking about Edwardian flâneurs or Georgian nature-poets. "That's quite different. There used to be one, don't you remember, who walked the whole length of the Banbury Road grinning at everyone, with an upright stick in his fist. Big red beard and staring eyes."

"Oh yes?" said Father Eustace.

"Stank like a polecat. Perfectly harmless."

Father Eustace smiled vaguely.

"I do perhaps remember him. And the one on Magdalen Bridge with his coat tied round the middle with string, always ready to talk with everybody about anything at all. Lovely man."

"I wouldn't have said lovely," frowned Graham.

"You said harmless," replied Father Eustace. "But where's the harm in the homeless? Who would choose to sleep in the streets?"

"No one is born in the streets," said Graham, knowing in his heart that he was now appearing offensive to the priest. "They bring it on themselves."

Father Eustace gave a little laugh as if to say: "I've heard that before and really don't need to answer it." He stared at a muddy footprint on the ground as if it held the secret answer to all life's problems. Effie, who had been snuffling in some bushes further up the lane, came back to him and looked up, impatiently wagging her tail.

"I'm wanted, I'm afraid," he said. "Better move on."

"Of course," said Graham. "Composing your next sermon as usual, are you? Do you take mental notes as you go along?"

"Yes," lied Father Eustace. He beamed at Graham benignly, as he would beam at a child caught teasing a cat, an expression of his infinite understanding of transgression and of his postponement of rebuke, it being too troublesome to interfere.

It was really none of his immediate business if Graham was so prejudiced.

He went on his way, and Graham was late for work.

No one is born in the streets, Graham repeated to himself. What quarrel with an unsympathetic father could lead to permanent exclusion? What carelessness with money and failure to keep up obligations could result in the loss of a home? He knew in theory of such things, of the loss of jobs and benefits, of the heartlessness of landlords, of the accumulating disappointments in the lives of the very poor. But he believed that society still provided a safety-net, and that his taxes paid for it. And after all, weren't they all really on drugs? That's why they begged. They needed money for drugs. They were losers, that was it. Losers. Most of them didn't even have the energy and resourcefulness to burgle houses to feed their foul habits.

But wasn't begging also a kind of theft? Instead of the violence of breaking and entering, the effrontery of making you feel shame. You wouldn't go around distributing money, would you? But if you were pestered for money you would be made to feel that you had to give something. That was extortion. Burgling and begging were both ways of making you conscious of what you possessed and conscious of the naturally unequal distribution of such possessions.

And why should he be ashamed of what he possessed? He had worked for it all his life and had inherited little from his family, but he hoped that he would have enough to provide for his children. He had been careful with money, saving and investing. Maddie's own money had made a difference to their life together, and though they had not lived on Boar's Hill, at least they hadn't had to live in Cowley. He couldn't expect any more from the Brigadier-General, and told himself, untruthfully, that he wouldn't accept any of it if it happened to come his way. The Brigadier-General could leave it directly to Susan and Michael if he wanted to, of course, and perhaps he would. But Graham felt (without at all thinking it through) that he wouldn't want it to amount to more than he was leaving them himself. That wouldn't be right at all.

In fact, Graham thought, Michael needed to pull himself together before he could be said to deserve to inherit anything. He thought of their last telephone conversation, where his son had ended up saying: "Dad, I don't think you've quite understood. I'm not coming 'home', as you put it. I've got a home here now."

Graham thought he understood perfectly well. Michael didn't want to be kept up to the mark. He wanted to escape so that he could do as he liked, and waste money as he had done on previous occasions when Graham had given him some.

"I know that, Michael. Of course, I know that you've got a place of your own. But Yarnfield Close will always be your home. Please don't forget it. Your room is still here."

"Of course, Dad, of course. But I can't come next Sunday."

"When can you come then? You tell me."

"I'll let you know. I will, I promise. And I want you to meet Koon-Mi. Just don't go on and on about it. And you can clear out the room if you really need to. There's nothing there I want to keep, except the chess magazines. I've got everything here now. You know that."

Graham had no idea what that "everything" might be. He remembered going in the car with Maddie to London, when Michael was first living out of the hostel and was sharing a house with some other third-year students. The car was crammed with boxes of stuff, but it still didn't seem more than a quarter of his possessions. Now he had his own "flat" in Barking, which seemed even smaller than his previous house-share. What did Michael's material life consist of? Graham had no idea. When he did venture into his son's room at Yarnfield Close, pausing thoughtfully in the doorway as he might do when visiting an interesting cathedral on holiday, he could only notice the clearly historical relics: the patiently-constructed Airfix model, the football stickers, the Linkin Park poster. The most sacred of them, the pastel bricks and the dinosaurs, had been long removed by Maddie to the attic. And now Maddie herself was gone, perhaps the last true worshipper.

Michael seemed to sense this, and treated his surviving parent as merely the secular caretaker of his place in the family, concerned only with practicalities.

He never came right out and said: "Dad, you need to get a life." But he clearly thought that Graham led an improperly reduced existence, as though he were not only a perhaps still-grieving widower, but somehow now demoted within the family, without a clear function. As though his authority had only been attained through Maddie, as though his love for Michael and Susan could only be validated by his access to them through her. Insofar as he was aware of this, Graham knew that with fathers it must always be so. His own father had elaborately deferred to his mother at every point, and Graham had despised him for it. When the great usurper, Lord Lymphoma, had taken his own rightful place in Maddie's life and then removed her altogether, he knew that in losing Maddie he must also lose Michael.

He didn't feel the same about Susan, with whom he had always felt a special relationship, particularly from the time of Michael's arrival when she started throwing jealous fits and he had been happy to take her side. He had been sorry when she had married Denzil Durfey and then moved to Cambridge, but thought that he had behaved very well about it, whereas Maddie had been interfering and quarrelsome for some reason. Susan was now happily settled, and Graham felt that he continued to represent the stability of the home she should be relaxed enough to come back to from time to time. But to Michael, Graham could be no substitute for his mother.

To Graham, Michael was in some strange way a potentially better version of himself. Would he not complete all that had been begun? Would he not proceed much further along the path which Graham had struggled to find? Was he not better educated? Would he not earn more? Would he not achieve greater recognition? And wouldn't Graham therefore be infinitely proud of him?

It didn't seem so. Not yet. "Dad, just don't go on and on about it!" Michael put him at a distance, and ignored his advice. When he might have come home to help him to pick up the pieces, he went off travelling. And Graham now had no idea what his prospects were at work. Michael simply wouldn't talk about it.

And Graham, not for the first time, had lost his temper and ended the call. Not in an obvious rage, but quietly, and without the customary fond farewells. Enough, he imagined, to leave

10

Michael still standing there, slightly puzzled, with the phone at his ear. And, he hoped, with regrets.

Of course, there was still his room at Yarnfield Close. It would always be his home.

Graham knew that he could lose his temper. It seemed to happen (and he allowed it to happen) much more often since he had lost Maddie. It was as though without her calming influence he could allow himself a greater natural expression of feeling without her implied rebukes. Thinking of her after some outburst, he would try to judge the matter impartially. "You should be more patient, Graham," she might have said. But he could always retort: "And let them trample all over you?" That would refer to her lack of real success in the musical world, and he had never liked to go down that road while she was alive. But now there was no one to tell him he might be wrong, or if obviously right, that he should keep quiet about it. Why keep quiet? There was too little plain speaking in the world.

He had spoken his mind only the other day in St. Giles'. A pale man with a hooded face and fingerless gloves was sitting against the wall outside the Taylorian, accompanied by a stout dog as savage as the man was thin and weak. He had chosen to sit there to give him immediate access to the Chinese tourists descending, hygienically masked, from their coloured coaches which had unlawfully stopped in the parking bays. This beggar, comfortably ensconced on folded cardboard and bedclothes, had claimed a public space as if by right. He would therefore be more or less the first thing that these visitors to Oxford would see when they arrived. He had taken it upon himself to represent his city as one which so neglected its citizens that they were compelled to ask foreigners for their bounty. In their forced pity for him, or in their embarrassment, they would part with the currency they still barely understood and later come to think ill of the city they had admired from afar, with its gargoyles, its gowns and its film locations. And it was all so false, so unnecessary! The man was begging to feed a habit.

As Graham passed, the man murmured something so indistinctly that he might have been speaking to his dog, or remembering a line of a poem.

"Change?" he said. Something about change.

11

Graham erupted.

He went over to the man and bent down towards him with a furious smile. From a distance he would have looked benevolent, as though about to drop some coins into his paper cup.

"*Change?*", said Graham. "You mean money, don't you? My money that I've earned by working. I don't suppose you know what working is, do you? So you want some of my money? Do you? I don't think so."

The man looked up at him without any obvious sense of affront, and whistled soundlessly with a slight wince, as though he were cooling his tea. His eyes flickered away for an instant to see if there were any witnesses to this gratuitous attack, but only the dog was near enough. It opened its wet mouth and appeared to laugh, with its tongue hanging out.

"And I certainly don't want to contribute to the upkeep of that dog," said Graham. "It must eat twice as much as you do."

The dog sucked the tongue back into its mouth and then settled with its head on its paws. It, or something, smelled of fish.

Graham straightened himself, then walked away without feeling any of the dignity that should have belonged to the position he had taken. Something conclusive was missing, he thought. The man supplied it.

"Have a very nice day, sir," he said, to Graham's retreating back.

How had it come to this? The man seemed as unconcerned as if he were behind the counter at a newsagent. Or a waiter, automatically pocketing a tip which he didn't deserve. Except of course that he had received nothing. That was the point, wasn't it? It didn't matter whether Graham gave him a pound or not, because he was not desperate, and soon enough someone would give him something, and all day long he would sit there, and the somethings would mount up, and at the end of the day he would be able to go and buy his fix.

If he were desperate, if it really mattered, he would behave quite differently. He would be urgently seeking help, and Graham knew he would be able to tell the difference.

The man, with his faint beard and evasive eyes, had made him think of Michael. What would Michael do if he were ever short of money? He would come home, wouldn't he, and ask his father for help? But what a terrible admission of failure that would be.

Getting a life, not in the dismissive idiomatic sense of the phrase which he had feared from Michael, but as a constructive path forward, was something that Susan sometimes seemed to have in mind for him, and to be hinting at on the rare occasions when she visited with the boys. She always brought with her the aura of the physical life satisfyingly led, and her criticisms could sound patronising.

"Who do you see, Dad?" she would ask. "And I don't mean at the Golf Club."

"I don't know who you can mean," he might reply. "Or what you mean. I have friends at work. Your mother's friends have lost interest in me."

"That can't be true, surely."

"Can't it? The Flints? The Ruskins? Even Caroline?"

"Goodness, I didn't suppose that Caroline would go on seeing just you. She was practically in love with Mum."

"The Flints, then?"

"They came at Christmas, didn't they?"

"That's different. Anyway, I have my own friends."

Graham's dismissive smile, guarded and not quite risking self-pity, was intended to put an end to such a conversation. The truth was that he didn't really have friends in the sense that Susan took a pride in, with her busy social life, colleagues at the library, circle of mothers, book group, college life through Denzil, and so on. Susan really knew this, but liked to persist. She was rightly suspicious of the claim that he had anyone who might truly be called his "own friend."

"You've got to make an effort, Dad. It's not as though you're a woman. I know a widow gets neglected by her husband's professional friends, when it was him they always really wanted to see."

"It happens to widowers, too."

The unspoken topic was in the air like the preparatory aromas of a meal to which you know you haven't been invited. Would

Graham be likely to go on living alone? If their old friends were neglecting him, what about new friends? Perhaps he might be "seeing" someone?

Not likely, thought Graham. And of course, Susan didn't think so either.

Sometimes he reviewed in his head the various fantasies that had afflicted him in the past. The thing with Mary Flint, for example, unspeakable even to himself. Temptations of a trivial nature, less frequent, oddly enough, since Maddie's death, and never very frequent at all. Liz at the department. Marian Peacock, for God's sake. All shaming, getting nowhere very much. He knew that he enjoyed female company, though, and missed it. And occasionally he went out of his way to seek it, and took pleasure from a degree of intimacy that he knew would go only so far and no further.

It was like that with Phyllis Jordan, his neighbour at no 1. He thought of her as a raffish single woman, once partnered, and with a strange life judging by the things that seemed to go on in her house: the number of people turning up in the evenings and clogging up the Close with their cars, for example, or a single younger man collecting her in an open car.

It was in the interests of half-intimacy (rather daring in a way, he told himself) that he had offered to mend Phyl's carriage clock. She had told him that it had stopped when he was delivering flyers for a charity event at the Golf Club. It was ten-ish in the morning, and the clock, impudent on the hall table, insisted on twenty past two.

She's only passing the time of day, he thought. A stopped clock isn't something she'd bother about at all. But once he'd taken it away, he reflected that it might have meant something to her after all, something like her life being put on hold.

Her house was much older than any of the others in Yarnfield Close, having been created by successive modernisations of what must have been an early Victorian stone cottage, perhaps built for some proprietor or guardian of the many fruit orchards and market gardens that had at one time operated north of the city. The Close had come later, carved out of the fields as the population expanded, with its entre-deux-guerres bungalows and brick villas, some of

14

them now also added to, with daring designer extensions and varied roof-pitches, and decorative garden trees creaking and top-heavy at the end of their natural lives. Though furthest from the alley towards the river, no. 1 had its own access to it, through a long garden that ran extravagantly behind the shorter fanned-out gardens of nos. 2 to 5. This garden seemed so wild and superfluous that it didn't give Phyllis Jordan quite the edge over the other residents of the Close that it might otherwise have done. She didn't seem proud of it. She didn't even seem to cultivate it.

O n occasions when Graham woke with a start from terrible dreams and found his chest fluttering, he vowed to make an appointment with his GP.

But he was immensely put off by the whole business when he found that Dr Driffield was a member of his Golf Club. He was accustomed, out of a mixture of fear and social deference, to calling his doctor "Dr Hartnett" or perhaps sometimes "doctor", and old Dr Hartnett's extremely profuse and wiry eyebrows had seemed to validate the formality. Not much had ever gone wrong with Graham himself, but naturally he had seen a lot of Dr Hartnett during Maddie's illness, and somehow the eyebrows had been a comfort. A man who let fierce eyebrows grow freely like that, and yet who still had time for a twinkle and a touch on the arm, was much to be respected.

But Dr Hartnett had now retired, and Graham was transferred to another doctor in the practice, Dr Paul Driffield. It soon became known, largely through neighbourly talk, that he liked to be called Paul. Or at least that he was very ready to be called Paul. This small revolution in the cause of social levelling was not to Graham's taste. You don't call doctors by their first names! But then, in the Golf Club bar Graham encountered him in a merry circle of old friends, Con Bullett the builder, his solicitor Henry Bradshaw, Bill Peacock and a few others, who were all calling him Paul.

Although he had consulted Paul Driffield at least once, on one occasion about a mole which was immediately pronounced to be harmless, Graham couldn't believe that his doctor would

15

remember him. And would it have mattered if he did? Perhaps he was Con's doctor as well. He might be doctor to half the members of the Club and their wives as well, and know all their secrets. This pale witty man nursing a strange reddish drink was surely not going to start publicly alluding to the various ailments of his drinking companions, but to call him Paul seemed to invite an intimacy whereby at some point, some private moment when teeing off or washing hands in the lavatory, his doctor might enquire about the development of symptoms or express some disapproval of his life-style, which would be nothing short of taking liberties. The Golf Club was above all the place where one went to escape from such matters. Or was Graham alone in fearing medical intimacy? Perhaps he was. But he really couldn't imagine Bill Peacock in the flush of achieving an eight-foot putt casually raising with Paul Driffield his prostate anxieties.

It was very tricky, Graham thought. You could keep things from "Dr Driffield" if you wanted to, but it would be harder to keep them from "Paul." And he much feared knowledge of his body in someone that he met socially, someone who was moreover much younger than himself.

When his blood-pressure was taken during his consequent visit to the surgery, it had to be taken several times, and was either so high or so inconsistent that he was given a monitor to carry home, with instructions about taking the pressure himself several times a day over the course of a week or so. A blood sample was also taken, so that Dr Driffield would find out something about such things as cholesterol levels, the state of his prostate, and liver and kidney function.

"I'm not an old man," Graham protested,

"Of course not," said Dr Driffield, typing into his computer. Graham wished that he could read what was being written. "Just think of it as an M. O. T. Your car has to have one after three years, and you wouldn't think of that as being old, would you?"

"Some people trade in their cars within three years," said Graham illogically, and then gave a little laugh when he realised what he had implied.

Dr Driffield looked up and smiled.

"There you go," he said. "You never know what your body is trying to tell you."

"I hope *you* know," said Graham.

"In most cases we can tell pretty quickly."

Dr Driffield had stopped typing, and swivelled his chair to face Graham.

"Would you say," he asked slowly, "that you are a naturally tense or anxious person?"

Graham didn't think that he was, and had never been asked such a question. He was momentarily embarrassed, feeling that it was a doctor's business to discover physical malfunctions, not to examine traits of character. Was he naturally tense? What had that got to do with anything? He decided to make another joke, a deliberate one this time.

"Aren't we all anxious these days?" he said. "With this wretched government and everything."

"Ah yes," said Dr Driffield. "The cut-backs. Quite."

Graham hadn't meant cut-backs at all. He was thinking of the failure to deliver Brexit. Was his doctor, who didn't seem to drink gin or scotch like everyone else, a lefty? That was another drawback to socializing with someone to whom you had to entrust your care. You could all too easily discover their own weaknesses.

Dr Driffield had discovered nothing immediately wrong, but suggested that in addition to the blood test, and to monitoring his own blood-pressure, Graham might care to make an appointment with the nurse for an ECG.

"And also, perhaps avoid reading the newspapers?"

Graham thought that their political difference might have profitably come into the open at this point. The man could hardly be a friend of Bill Peacock's or Con Bullett's, could he? But he could think of nothing appropriate to say, and left.

H e took the carriage clock back to Phyllis Jordan, who looked at it with a little whoop of delight.

"You've got it to go again already? Oh, how kind," she said.

Graham smiled at her. He expected her to ask how he had managed it. He wanted to be able to play down the trouble it had been, the search for an appropriate key, the opening of the case, the easing of the spring, the breaking of the spring, the eventual visit to a clock-maker in Kidlington. He wanted to be thought calm, efficient and off-hand. He wanted her delight to prompt further and further questions, and further and further praise, which would then be put to one side with a modest smile. But she seemed to take it all somewhat for granted.

"What a handyman you are. Would you like a coffee?"

"Aren't you busy?"

"No, that's fine."

Graham was under the impression that she worked from home in some way, running something like a social web-site. He didn't know where in the rest of her unusually large house her office might be, or whether she kept hours there as though under invisible supervision. The parts that he could see were in disarray.

They drank their coffees at the kitchen table, looking up the local house prices in Zoopla. She said she found them appalling, though she was clearly excited by them. The clock was not forgotten, but the dramatic story of its laborious mending was now lost for ever.

"Well over a million?" she queried, rolling her eyes.

"It's unbelievable," he agreed.

"What does it make this worth?" she said, nodding around her kitchen.

He looked at the tiers of open shelves, the chipped work surface, the rusted handle and lock of the door to the outside pantry.

"Yes," he said. "A goldmine."

At least it had the outside pantry. And the mossy brick outbuildings around it, none of which his own newer house had. He remembered even seeing an old mangle among the junk there, and Maddie, who used to call on Phyl quite often, had been critical of the way she lived, distant as a lady of the manor, subscribing to two newspapers, getting Ocado deliveries, but careless in her habits, the cat eating off the table, the lavatory sometimes

18

unflushed and so on. Graham suspected that they used to talk politics, and avoided asking Maddie questions later.

Phyl's house was indeed in a bit of a state, but he supposed that being as large as it was it had potential. That was the thing. Not the condition, but the size. After all, that immense side garden was the size of a building plot. With planning permission, she could make a lot of money. That's what he would have done himself. Actually, her house must be worth a very great deal.

But when he suggested it as a possibility, she dismissed it.

"There are too many houses here already," she said. "We need all the green space we can get."

Graham thought that if it was green space she wanted she could make better use of it. It was a wilderness, not a garden; an accumulation of forgotten areas, crumbling walls and neglected orchard, culminating in a half-collapsed fence along the lane at the back, tilted beneath the weight of overgrown elder. It was very likely the meeting-place of those druggies that he had heard quarrelling. Had she heard anything?

"No," she said. "But I don't suppose I would do, would I?"

Was this meant to be because of her involvement with her work, or the physical distance of her house from the lane and the river? Damp coffee rings, and older dry ones, not only on the strewn newspapers but on some unopened letters, spoke of slovenliness rather than preoccupation with more important matters. He didn't think that anything much in her life seemed to be very important. But perhaps her work was all-absorbing, and he knew nothing about that.

"There was that boy, though, the other day," she added.

"What boy?

"It was rather strange. He came to the door asking me if I would fill up his bottle with water."

"With water?"

"Yes."

"What sort of bottle?"

"A sort of big beer bottle. You know, with a wired stopper and a rubber washer. Why?"

"I don't know. Why should he want water?"

"I presumed he was thirsty. I don't think he needed it for a car."

"What did he look like?"

"I didn't really notice."

"No?"

"Well, the usual sort of clothes. A grey sort of jerkin. Track-suit bottoms. A bit dirty."

"Dirty?"

"You know. A bit rough. Very thin, actually. Why are you quizzing me about him?"

"Am I?" Graham didn't want to make her uncomfortable, but something made him persist. "And you filled his bottle for him?"

"Well, yes," she said. "Of course."

"You want to be careful, you know," Graham went on. "Where was he going?"

"Going? He didn't say."

"Perhaps he wasn't going anywhere. Perhaps he'll come back."

"Oh, I shouldn't think so."

"A young tramp."

"It was a warm day."

Somehow the atmosphere of neighbourly good deeds and the shared interest in the excessive value of their houses had dissipated. The half-inch of coffee in Graham's cup was cold, and he soon took his leave.

"Not to worry," he said frankly, with a little touch of her shoulder that didn't mean anything, but perhaps wasn't (he felt) intended to mean nothing. And Phyl never seemed to worry about anything at all.

Yes, why should anyone worry about anything? The usual rains of June, unexpected but recognized, had finished at last, and there was a balminess in the air. When he was doing some pruning in the garden at the week-end, he could hear Marian and Bill talking over the hedge next door and thought they sounded unusually jolly even for them. He could hear a motor mower from across the Close. A pigeon was doing some rough wooing from a lilac nearby, stopping in mid-cadence as if taken by a sudden thought.

Graham smiled. All's right with the world, he reflected. But he was aware of himself thinking it, as if in quotation marks (and it was a famous quotation, wasn't it?) and so he was immediately wary of it. Nothing was ever quite right in his experience. He was learning to live with his loss, and what he did have left sometimes seemed to be slipping through his fingers.

He made himself a coffee, and sat down with a list of things to be done. It always made him feel better, this mapping of the future life. He knew it would make him feel better, even though the tasks might stay uncompleted, and even though the listing of them brought a slight intolerance or rebelliousness of the spirit at the prospect of bringing them to completion. The lists were kept in a little notebook that lived in his bed-side drawer.

There were things he could cross off, like "Phyl's clock", and there were perennial items, like "clear pod", "BP monitor" and even "clear attic" that were on-going. That left:

"Shop for Michael"

"Police—needle"

"Con—find Saver Account"

The second of these he could do straight away, and he did it from his mobile, while his coffee was still comfortingly warm. But the police didn't seem interested at all in the needle, even when he explained that there were children living in the Close who played in the lane and the fields by the river, and who might be harmed by it. Did he want to make a complaint, he was wearily asked? He could imagine the sergeant at the other end of the phone, with files of existing complaint questionnaires in front of him, not wanting to have to fill out any more. Graham soon realised that there was nothing he could actually complain about, and after a sharp remark about the police cuts, he eventually ended the call.

He had made many such calls in the past, and was known for making them. They ranged from complaints about orange hire bikes left on the pavements ("Better there than in the canal, sir") to alarmist reports of weapons found in the Close ("These are Swat Mission Die Cast Cap guns, sir. They are toys. My son has one."). As soon as he had given his name, he was aware of the ensuing pause at the other end of the line that was long enough to conceal a sigh. Well, he was unrepentant. Someone had to keep an eye on things. Someone had to keep things up to the mark.

He would shop for Michael's visit on Tuesday and make up the beds later. Graham knew very well that Michael and Koon-Mi would want to sleep together in the big spare room bed, and whatever he thought about that likelihood the room would have to be prepared for Koon-Mi anyway, even were Michael in fact to sleep in his own old room. Graham knew that Michael was now an adult, but somehow he did not feel that to be quite the case. And in one small corner of his mind there was a perplexing confusion of sexual jealousy which he had no intention of confronting at all.

This left the Saver Account details, which really should be found without delay, for hadn't Con Bullett spoken of a deadline at the end of the month?

"No leeway, Graham my old mate," he had said. "On my desk by the 30th, or it won't work. Hard deadline. Hard as Brexit."

Con Bullett was the local builder who had started a company to develop what he had described to Graham (and no doubt to many another crony at the Golf Club and elsewhere) as a "simply brilliant blue-chip money-spinner." The idea was to produce tiny living units for boutique hotels or for mass accommodation of any kind, linked to airports or universities, for example.

"Instant rooms," he had explained. "You could fit at least two into any ordinary room so that even your local B & Bs could double, perhaps treble, in size with minimum conversion costs. It's a winner. The Japanese are doing it. Why shouldn't we do it?"

He had taken Graham with a dozen others to inspect his prototype. There was an offer of shares to the privileged few, which would certainly (much like the capacity of those B & Bs) triple in value once the company had gone public. Con appeared to mention the figure at which it was certain the shares would be quoted next month on the Stock Exchange, and it was indeed decidedly more than the price at which he was now offering them at to his favoured friends (£35 a share). Con asked Debbie to hand out copies of the illustrated brochure. The way he pronounced "brochure" made it sound like an expensive cream pastry.

Graham was impressed by both the prototype and the look of the brochure, although the prototype did feel a little like a cross-channel ferry cabin with some unusual moulded fittings, and when he later read the brochure he could find no financial information among the rosy smiling faces of the residents of the new living units, which were called "Bullettpods." Con had supplied an additional form of application for the shares, which could be completed on-line with a BACS payment (or by post, with a cheque if Graham preferred). It appeared that you could acquire them in multiples of 100. No small investment, then.

Graham was no fool. He knew that there was no guarantee that he would make any money out of Bullettpods. But he knew Con well enough, and knew that his business was flourishing. Half the old Victorian houses in North Oxford, until quite recently seedy assemblages of student digs or hastily-converted annexes of language colleges, were being bought up, brickwork scrubbed clean, equipped with nanny-extensions and basement swimming-pools and electronically gated. This was the sort of work that Con was good at, and it was bringing in millions from the foreign oligarchs who were happy to sit back and let him do everything.

There were other factors that swayed Graham. He had heard of the designer, or thought he had, and looked him up on-line to check. This fellow had an Italian name and had won awards for light-weight collapsible furniture. He also had some impressive-looking letters after his name, though Graham had no idea what any of them stood for. And Graham had this old Saver Account at his building society which when he was younger had seemed to serve as a nice little addendum to his future pension, and over twenty years it had mounted up, of course. But what was once something like 5% interest had been slowly downgraded to .5%, and he had never done anything about it.

Still, it was a sizeable sum doing absolutely nothing, not even keeping pace with inflation. Worth a gamble? He now had Maddie's investment portfolio, transferred to him intact after her death, not to mention the proceeds of her cello, and that would now cover many a rainy day. And finally, thinking of Maddie, he was intrigued by the name "Bullettpods." When she had bought her own pod, it was marketed as such, though Graham had complained that for the price it seemed little more than a glorified garden shed, though soundproofed, and with an electricity extension included in the price.

Now it had become a kind of shrine to her memory, and the word pod was itself part of the memory, a very female word after all. Hadn't Maddie always proudly claimed, in the exalted flush of her early motherhood, that Susan had simply popped out of her, like a pea from a pod?

Graham took to the idea of Bullettpods for all these reasons, and also, if he had bothered to interrogate his own mind further, because the word suggested the impregnable aura of "bullet-proof" and he had liked the afternoon sunlight falling on the fine gold hairs of Debbie's fore-arm as she handed out the brochures.

He went into town to close the Saver Account, and was met with what he considered to be an outrageous obtuseness. For sums of that size it was apparently necessary that he submit the request in writing, with the original paperwork setting up the account and two pieces of identification. Only then could the balance be computed with up-dated interest (interest at .5%!) and transferred to his current bank account. He was livid, and took it out on the young cashier who he was convinced was mistaken.

"You can always ask to see the manager, sir," said the cashier.

Graham was aware that there was a queue behind him, and didn't want to incur general displeasure at further delay.

"I expect your manager is as much of an idiot as you are," he hissed, with a smile, at the thick protective glass between him and his victim, and stalked out with a triumphant nod at the uninterested customers.

Did he still have all that paperwork? He supposed so, since he was careful about such things. But he put off looking straight away since he was afraid that he wouldn't find it in the first place he looked. It was quite likely to be somewhere else.

It was a mistake to have taken his blood pressure that afternoon. He sat at the table with a cup of tea. The by now familiar groan of the monitor and the bullying squeeze of his arm was the opposite of reassuring. In fact, he was doubly irritated. His BP was 187/80.

Things that are lost are never really lost, thought Graham. The little boy who goes missing turns out to have been somewhere all the time. Somebody's son. Even if he's died, in Syria perhaps, he was there when it happened, although no one knew about it. He remembered his son-in-law Denzil telling him about the number of missing books in the Cambridge University Library.

"People presume they've been stolen, of course, but it's actually quite difficult to steal books from a library that doesn't lend them. No, it's just that they've been misplaced. A reader orders a book by submitting a shelf-mark. The book is found and brought to the distribution desk. The reader collects it, takes it to his own desk, and later returns it. All well and good. But then, if the fool assistant with all these books on her trolley that readers have finished with returns any of them to the wrong place on the shelf, or even to the wrong shelf, especially to the wrong shelf, it can't be found next time, do you see, and will be reported missing."

"Ah," Graham had said, "like a soldier in wartime."

"Indeed," was Denzil's reply, as he rolled his bread into little pieces and nibbled at them with his yellow teeth. "Everyone thinks 'dead', do you see, but the chap simply hasn't reported for duty. Nine times out of ten, he's taken the recent engagement as an opportunity to scarper. He's in the wrong place. The book is in the wrong place. It might be the only copy in the country, and nobody can ever read it again."

"Why 'her' trolley?" Susan had asked.

"What?"

"You presume that it's women library assistants who are incompetent."

Denzil had given a little ascending falsetto laugh.

"Don't let's start on all that again," he smiled.

It had been one of those times when the boys were quite little, and his daughter had wanted to bring them to Oxford to be shown off to their grandparents. Graham remembered it as much for the evidence that Denzil was a tweed-waistcoated twerp as for the point about misplaced books. It wasn't the first time he had thought so, but he and Maddie had had an interesting conversation about it afterwards. "Susan worked in the Bodleian for a time," she had reminded him. "He's an idiot."

At the time Graham had been shocked to discover that he was now meant to think of his distinguished son-in-law as an idiot. Denzil Durfey was described as a philosopher in the newspapers, even when he was writing reviews of books about abortion or animal rights. He must therefore be a lover of wisdom, mustn't he? Could a professional lover of wisdom also be an idiot? But Maddie was always right.

Graham had looked for the original correspondence that had set up the Saver Account in the box-file of his investment reports, the obvious place, he thought. But it wasn't there. He knew that he was always refiling papers, and never quite deciding where they belonged—receipts, bills, things to do with the house, tax stuff, it all overlapped in his mind. Yes, the correspondence must be somewhere, and the analogy with Denzil's story of the *Fragments of Oesetes of Nisiros*, lost to present scholarship though known to exist in a rare edition (Antwerp, 1523) was in a way encouraging. His filing system was nothing like the vast Cambridge Library.

But at the back of his mind he couldn't help thinking of those soldiers "missing" in war. Surely Denzil had been wrong about that. The missing did usually turn out to be dead after all, didn't they? Everybody knew it as a euphemism. So missing papers might well turn out to have been thrown away by mistake. He would look more thoroughly later.

He had Michael's visit to think about.

Edging his car out backwards into the road to go to the supermarket, he waved cheerily to the man from Grangers who was mowing those front lawns of the Close that were open and adjacent. This wasn't garden held in common, but since a majority of the houses had front gardens of this type they clubbed together to pay the firm for their upkeep, and payment was arranged through the Association. The noise of the mower, frequent in the summer months, was an attractive feature of life in the Close, indicating by its devoted murmur a keeping up of appearances in the best sense.

There were two figures, male and female, walking into the Close on the other side of the road. They were thin young people of indeterminate age, and he supposed that they might be friends of the Terry children. It was only as he was driving away, still just able to see them in his rear-view mirror, that he noticed that the boy was wearing a grey hoodie.

Was it the same one that had called at Phyl's house asking for water? Were they the pair he had heard arguing beyond his fence? He thought of turning the car around by reversing in Crossland Road and returning to the Close, but guessed that they would have passed through the alley into the lane by then, and he would have lost them. He was disturbed by their continued presence.

His shopping distracted him. He was looking forward to Michael's visit, and to meeting Koon-mi. The fact that Michael had a Korean girl-friend had energised Graham in some way that he didn't quite understand. There had been things about his son in the past that he hadn't understood either (the chess, for example, or his weird A Level choices that had done him no favours) but there had always been Maddie on hand to point out the pros, in that calm reasonable way of hers, when he could only see the cons. Now he couldn't talk with Maddie about Koon-Mi. He was on his own with this one, and was both disapproving and excited. Michael was still surely too young to think of getting married, and wasn't there something gauche about him, something unfinished, some lack of drive, that meant that he should be concentrating on a career rather than acquiring a partner (as girl-friends seemed rather prematurely to be called these days)? That was patently true, but at the same time this Korean girl sounded like an exotic trophy, and Graham was lost in wonder at why she should have attached herself to his son.

There was a Far eastern cabinet at the supermarket where Graham was pleased to find ready-to-steam prawn dumplings and fresh noodles. The vegetable aisles had bean sprouts and pak choi, and elsewhere he found jars of Thai green curry sauce. He had no idea what Korean food was like. Was it pretty much like Chinese food, or was it more like Japanese? There were some Japanese cartons there as well, quite mysterious to Graham, as they were nothing like sushi, which he knew about but didn't like. And Miso soup, in little sachets. That would all be easy enough. He would cook all this on their first evening, and take them out on the following day, perhaps to Brown's, or the Golf Club.

Coming out of the supermarket he gave a wide berth to the cheerful seller of *The Big Issue*, but encountered a young woman cyclist riding towards him on the broad pavement between the parked cars and the decorative tubs of shrubs. Grinning at her challengingly, he held his arms out widely in a gesture that from a short distance looked like a greeting, because she stopped clumsily, putting out her foot to balance, and smiled back in puzzlement. Was this someone she should know?

"Not on the pavement," said Graham. "We don't cycle on pavements."

His first-person plural must have lent him for a moment a schoolmasterly air of authority, for the woman, instead of cursing him as perhaps she was minded to do, shook her head in irritation and disbelief and wobbled away around him.

"It's in the Highway Code," Graham sang out after her. "Stupid!"

On his return he made a determined effort to find the stuff about his Saver Account, and did eventually find it. Always in the last place you look, he said to himself, adding the joke he had usually made to Maddie when she lost things: it's because you don't go on looking once you've found it. He also scanned on his printer his latest council tax bill and the appropriate pages of his passport, and put all the papers in the hall, ready for his visit to the Building Society.

A satisfying day, all in all. His blood pressure was 154/81.

Graham couldn't understand why the week-end wasn't quite the success he had expected. He had told himself in advance that he shouldn't interrogate Michael about his job and his prospects, and he thought he'd pretty well kept to that wise resolve. Michael looked thin and tired, and he clearly hadn't troubled to shave for several days. Graham said something about it at one point, which was obviously a mistake.

Koon-Mi was a disappointment and a puzzle. He had somehow envisaged a slim demure girl in a silk embroidered dress with a high collar, like one of the wives in *The King and I*. But she was small and quite stocky, wearing glasses and a t-shirt that said BORIS IS A BIG GIRL'S BLOUSE across the front. Graham didn't quite understand this, though he knew it was an insult. But a t-shirt is a sort of blouse, and if you look like a big girl yourself, why draw attention to it? He didn't care all that much about Boris Johnson one way or another, but it made him feel unsettled.

Koon-Mi also had a rather deep and knowing laugh, which at times (as when Michael put down COLON for 43 in their after-supper game of Scrabble) slightly irritated him. She is my guest here, he thought, and it's not her place to remind us of bodily functions. In his momentary embarrassment he pronounced:

"If the grate be empty, put some coal on!"

"Sorry?" said Koon-Mi.

"Oh, you've really no need to apologise," said Graham, quickly turning to Michael and adding: "You remember that saying of Granny's, don't you, Michael?"

When Michael shook his head, Graham wrote it down on the score pad: "If the B mt put some :"

"If the great B empty, put some coal on," he explained.

"Oh yes," Michael nodded. "A rebus."

"It's a mark of punctuation," Graham explained to Koon-Mi.

Koon-Mi sniggered again, and went on to beat them all by eighty points.

The meal hadn't been a success, either. He overcooked the chicken pieces he had unfrozen, and the soy sauce stuck to the pan. The beansprouts had turned to mush before the onions had cooked, and since he didn't know how to steam anything he had done the dumplings in the oven. They were hard and shrunken.

Michael and Koon-Mi were very polite about it, which only infuriated Graham. Why couldn't they be honest, and they could have had a laugh about it?

"Not what you're used to, I'm sure," he had said.

He and Michael had had words together in the kitchen when drying the dishes. Graham had cleared up, and was happily giving a professional buff to a wine glass when Michael said: "Did you really get rid of Mrs Liver?"

"I did," said Graham.

"But you don't do all the cleaning yourself, do you?"

Michael was taking in the state of the kitchen floor and work surfaces, and trying to be diplomatic. He had noticed that the whole house was in a bit of a mess.

"I'm quite able to do the housework," Graham said. "I can make beds. I can operate the washing machine, and I use the dry-cleaners for their shirt service."

"But what was wrong with Mrs Liver? Mum used to do so much in the house anyway. Why should you get rid of Mrs Liver as well? There must be an enormous amount to do."

Graham managed not to answer the question. He didn't much like the question itself. Getting rid of Mrs Liver *as well?* What did that mean? He hadn't got rid of Maddie! Michael could be so insensitive sometimes. No, Graham had never liked their cleaner, who he had once found sitting down having a coffee with Maddie instead of getting on with her work. He had suspected that Maddie talked to her about him. He could imagine her saying "Oh yes, you know what husbands are like" and unconsciously betraying him in all sorts of little ways. He really didn't like having Mrs Liver in the house at all, imagining that she poked her nose into his things. With Maddie no longer there, Mrs Liver would have every opportunity to satisfy her curiosity while he was at work, and then talk about him to all the other people she worked for. No, he wasn't having it. He had certainly got rid of Mrs Liver.

"Well, it's your choice," said Michael. "But I don't see why you should have to do everything. It's a lot of work. And the meal: I really don't know why you went to all that trouble."

"Oh, it was no trouble," Graham replied. "I thought it would be appropriate."

"Appropriate!" returned Michael, as though his father had delivered some racist slur. "And why did you say 'Not what you're used to'? Dad, Koon-Mi's British. She was born in Wolverhampton."

On Sunday morning they went to church. Even the free-spirited Koon-Mi made no objection, and Graham was relieved to see that Michael had, as requested, managed to persuade her to cover up her t-shirt, even though she had covered it with an old

30

cardigan with holes in the sleeves. He knew that Michael would be docile enough about going, because it was his mother's church, and the ritual was understood to be a way of acknowledging Maddie's absence. Graham wanted to go so that some sort of behavioural family guidelines might be laid down for Koon-Mi's benefit. He knew nothing about Korean religion, and didn't want to ask for fear of being accused again of racism.

In any case, he thought it would be useful to hear Father Eustace's sermon, so that he could talk to him about it at the Association's summer party. He always felt that there were aspects of theology, particularly when it touched on social issues, that were surprisingly easy to understand, and he believed that Father Eustace enjoyed defending his points of view. Graham certainly quite enjoyed trying to argue with him, since neighbours could always make jokes or turn the conversation to something else if things got tricky. During the sermon he glanced at Koon-Mi, hoping that she was impressed. She seemed to be in a trance. Perhaps the Korean religion was a mystical religion? Being in God's House could have that effect on people.

Father Eustace's text was taken from Matthew 24.43: "Watch therefore: for ye know not what hour your Lord doth come." The priest smiled upon them from his pulpit, raising his hands above his head as if to invite there and then the Second Coming of Christ which, as he went on to explain, though once historically expected as a certain millennial event was really, like most articles of belief, more like a state of mind.

"Matthew knew this very well," proclaimed Father Eustace, "since he continues with a parable that is affecting to all of us who are householders. He says: 'But know this, that if the goodman of the house had known in what watch the thief would come, he would have watched, and would not have suffered his house to be broken up. Therefore be ye also ready: for in such an hour as ye think not the Son of man cometh.' Be ye also ready! This is the message that Matthew has for us. The goodman of the house must be vigilant, and we in our souls must be vigilant too.

"Don't think that being good or doing good is enough. That isn't what it means when he singles out 'the goodman of the house.'

The Latin tells us more clearly. My friends, you will have to look tolerantly on me for speaking the language of learning in these troubled times in the university city of Oxford. The common mind which worships reason has forbidden it as elitist, you see. But the common minds which worship reason also believe that reason is enough, that being good or doing good is enough, and are not prepared to receive Christ into their souls. The Latin says: 'si sciret paterfamilias qua hora fur venturus esset, vigilaret utique et non sineret perfodi domum suam.' The goodman is not necessarily a good man, but is a 'paterfamilias', father of a household, who will keep the door well bolted. Reason is like a lock, a purely mechanical process, and again it is not enough. We also as householders need the watchfulness in our souls which the holy communion brings to us."

There was much more of this. Graham, who would have admitted that he didn't really know at all what a soul might be, was nonetheless taken with the idea of the soul as a house. He was proud of having a house. He was proud of having paid off the mortgage. He was proud of having raised two children in it. He knew it was something worth protecting. He liked to think of himself as a "goodman."

On their way out, with Koon-Mi embarrassing him by biting one of her sleeves like a teenager, Graham noticed his wife's friend Caroline Boxwood edging towards him, eyebrows raised in an exaggerated mime of greeting. After they had all acknowledged Father Eustace at the door (who insisted on putting his hands on Michael's shoulders and beaming on him as though he were a returned prodigal) they gathered outside awkwardly. Caroline intended to kiss all of them, though Michael mistimed his reluctant cheek.

"Such a brilliant man," she exclaimed loudly. "He'll be a bishop, you'll see!"

The sun was shining on the congregation as they drifted away in groups. Caroline asked Koon-Mi about her job, staring at her admiringly and giving little repeated nods of encouragement as though she deserved a prize for speaking at all. Graham felt relieved that Koon-Mi was being accepted so naturally, as if Caroline as Maddie's very old friend were somehow Maddie's proxy, and he glanced at Michael, hoping that he too was pleased. Michael still hadn't shaved, not even for church, but Graham hadn't dared to say anything to him about it. He didn't look pleased about anything, but glowered in the sun like a member of an audience reluctantly called up into the footlights.

"Why is Jesus a thief?" he said suddenly.

Caroline and Koon-Mi both broke off and looked at him, and Koon-Mi delivered the deep snigger that seemed to be her reaction to almost everything.

"Ah, Michael," said Caroline fondly. "You always had a very logical mind."

"It doesn't make sense," persisted Michael.

"Does anything?" said Caroline placatingly. "You'd better have it out with Father Eustace."

They were moving away from each other now, in their natural orbits of parting, and soon made their farewells. Caroline called brightly and inconsequentially after them:

"All my babies have beards, too!"

E ach day after work, Graham would take the pod keys from their hook in the kitchen and visit Maddie's shrine at the bottom of the garden. That oak rectangle, with its ecologically correct "living" roof, a just-visible mossy crust with the occasional fern and cornflower, was not only very Maddie, it was also like a coffin. Within it, because of the expensive and effective sound-proofing, the plunging arpeggios of Bach or the keening melodies of Elgar had erupted unheard. Michael, in the happier days of his Physics A Level, had compared his mother's cello to Schrödinger's Cat. "You don't know if she's playing or not, and when you open the door you still won't know, because she will have stopped," he said. "Or was not playing anyway, if you see what I mean." In those days, Graham was entirely proud of Michael, believing him to be clever in inverse proportion to his own failure to quite understand anything his son said. Now, when he unlocked and slid open the door, he could imagine that the mournful music had just at that moment ceased, and that a familiar face would look up at him, mouthing the question "Tea?" and smiling in forgiveness at being interrupted.

He had sold the cello without sentimental misgivings, believing that the expense of renewing the insurance premium was something to be prudently avoided. It was a 19th century Mirecourt instrument that Maddie had believed to be a Vuillaume, but real Vuillaumes were all numbered, he was told. He had many sleepless nights over the fact that he got less for it than its last insurance valuation. Typical of Maddie's wishful impracticality! If she had been alive he would have had it out with her, but as it was he had to take it on the chin.

Other related items, like the music stands, were eventually brought back to the house for disposal. He also removed the air-conditioning unit that had been necessary to counter the stuffiness of the pod in the summer, and it now did service in the bedroom. There wasn't much else that couldn't be left in the pod as appropriate furnishing for such a place and its possible further uses, but there was the question of Maddie's little chest of drawers in which she had kept her music. It was a good piece, Georgian, and had come from the Priory. Graham didn't know whether to have it valued and sell it, or simply leave it where it was. There were two small drawers, one locked, above the full-width drawers which contained the sheet music, and after a long period of agony and superstition he had located the key among Maddie's personal possessions.

It was his intention to open the locked drawer, but it was an intention postponed. He would stand there, doing nothing, or he would perhaps take a little vase back to the house and return it with a single rose, as if by doing so there were something outside himself that he could involve in his feelings. He supposed it was a sort of act of worship.

Then he could go back again to the kitchen for a well-deserved scotch.

The boy in the tracksuit was not in his mind at all when he answered the door one evening, but there indeed he stood, and for a moment Graham faced the figure on his doorstep with a neutral smile of enquiry as though it had been a delivery or a neighbour.

"I don't suppose you can lend me a pen, can you?"

The request was made in an entirely reasonable tone, one that made it apologetically clear that his lack of a pen was a misfortune that might fall upon anyone, that he was hardly to blame for not having one, and that of course it was a tribute to the civilised oasis that was Yarnfield Close that any of its householders (chosen at random as well as at need) could be presumed to possess one. Indeed, to possess many, so that one of them would not only be readily at hand, but might not even be missed, should there prove to be no convenient opportunity for the insignificant borrowed object to be returned. An object not perhaps quite as insignificant as water, it flashed through Graham's conflicted mind, but in the same category of readily dispensed charity to passing vagrants.

The conflict was between immediate angry dismissal, a default reaction in Graham's case, and a relaxed emulation of his neighbour's readiness to fill his bottle on a warm day. He hadn't really argued with Phyl about her unguarded generosity, knowing that if he had done so she might well have thought ill of him. And this now left him feeling that to comply with this ridiculous and presumptuous request might in fact be the best way to get rid of the stranger. He could send him satisfied on his way, as though the inhabitants of the Close might have already agreed on this course of action as likely to prevent a deteriorating situation, whereby a stranger might take offence and deliver curses, or spit on the doorstep. This, he remembered, had happened with cold-calling salesmen that Bill Peacock had explained were proved to have links with organised crime. It was better, Bill said, not to answer the door at all. But Graham has already answered the door!

The young man was younger than Michael, drawn and unshaven. But there was nothing abject or craven in his manner, and he showed no awareness that he was begging. He was asking for a pen in the way that any one of Graham's neighbours might have asked for a pen. He needed a pen, and didn't happen to have one on him. Silly, really. Could Graham oblige?

A rollerball had hardly any value. It wasn't going to be sold for drug money. Graham bought them in packets of ten at a time. They were always lying around, with the crossword, by the telephone, wherever. He was not only taken aback, but was caught entirely off-guard. And there was something about the casual presumption of the request which made it so entirely reasonable that Graham abandoned his first thought of a withering refusal and went into the kitchen to find one.

"There you go," he said, utterly surprised at himself.

"Cheers," said the young man

Graham realised from the confident idiom of gratitude that this filthy stranger, this vagrant prowler of the neighbourhood, an evident drug-dealer, the whiner he had heard over the fence, wasn't after all the lowest of the low, but perhaps of more uncertain social origins. Perhaps he was even a sort of tramp writer like that one who wrote about the hop pickers and waiters spitting in the soup, whatever he was called. They'd done him at school. No, not very likely. But why should he want a pen?

That evening his blood pressure was 190/69

There were times when Graham wondered what it would be like to lose his mind. He would stand in the middle of his living room not knowing why he had come in there when the moment before he had been sitting in the kitchen. He must have come to fetch something, but he had no idea what it was.

What had he just been doing? Oh yes, collecting newspapers and other bits of print that had accumulated in the kitchen, expensive freebie brochures, A5 envelopes that had contained unwanted invitations to part with his money, that sort of thing. He was doing the recycling. But hadn't he cleared the living room earlier? He went back into the kitchen to finish the job.

His indecision about opening Maddie's locked drawer was making him restless. He turned instead to kitchen cupboards, and shouted cheerfully to Liz Sherwood when he met her at the front with the blue recycling bin ("Never too late for a bit of spring cleaning!") and dumped plastic bags of useless and broken utensils into the landfill. Liz had smiled encouragingly ("I wish I could get Colin to do that!") and waved him on as though he were running a marathon.

He came inside, and returned to the living room to pick up the thread of his intentions. The emptiness of the room seemed like a rebuke to the emptiness of his life. Only these small domestic routines defined it.

The photographs on the mantelpiece grinned cheerfully at him from their silver frames. Maddie and her sister, Maddie with Caroline, Susan at college, Susan and Denzil at the Manoir at their ridiculously expensive wedding. His parents in Lanzarote. Susan and the boys shadowed in studio soft-focus. The faces seemed remote, even defiant. They were not really looking at him but at someone hired to instruct them in a pose, someone who was being paid for it. And all these also defined the emptiness of his life.

He could pretend that he had come into the room to look at Susan with little Tim and Rodney. He hadn't seen them in reality since Christmas, and when he had suggested that they might drive over and would be very welcome at the Close Association party, Susan had immediately said no, there was a college dinner. There was always something. The truth was, Graham knew very well that they couldn't be bothered with the journey and that Denzil hated coming. Denzil had once even made some impenetrable biblical joke in his presence about the wilderness of the forty roundabouts between Cambridge and Oxford or something. It didn't prevent them driving quite frequently to Scotland, which really was a wilderness in Graham's opinion.

Public photographs were impersonations, but family photographs contained secrets. He found boxes of old ones in the attic when he continued with his half-hearted clearances. They were still in the yellow envelopes in which they had been collected from the developers. There they all were, those holidays. Susan and Michael somewhere by the sea, gazing out from those frozen moments when someone had decided that they were meant to be happy and had pressed the shutter.

What these forgotten photographs told him now was that he had been quite wrong about the children. He had been living with the idea that Susan was the reliable and responsible one, who would always be tender to him, as she had been when she liked to comb his hair and deliver her hairdresser monologues, and that

Michael was a scamp, a tearaway who never tidied his room, ready to rebel as he believed boys always did.

But in these old snaps of childish postures and rivalries he suddenly saw the truth. The strutting Susan at Eastbourne and the anxious Michael at the Zoo were the true harbingers of their adult selves. It was Susan who had eagerly contrived a life distant from him, and Michael who was in fact ready to come home, however much he might theoretically protest. He suddenly saw his son's silence or criticism as insecurity and involvement, an ongoing need to connect with his father on any terms. Susan was just not there.

It must be true. Hadn't Michael telephoned after his recent visit to talk about the proposed investment? Graham had wanted to boast about his unique opportunity to make a killing with Bullettpods, and they had chatted about it at breakfast. Koon-Mi had said that they sounded "really really cool", but Michael had typically not said very much. However, when he rang the following day it was to issue a warning ("Dad, do you really want to get landed with this? Suppose you find you can't sell the shares? Is it guaranteed? I wouldn't get into it. Is it even legal?") and Graham had been put on the defensive. But he had to admit that this elaborate concern was touching. He couldn't imagine Susan taking any interest in it whatsoever. What interest she did show in his life seemed to be entirely concerned with whether or not she might in the future be required to act as his carer. She would like to set him up and forget about him, he thought. Rather as he had done with his own mother.

One box of photos led to another. Soon he was back to his own childhood, looking for images of his father, who never seemed to be on any of them. Had his mother really kept him in his place, and if so, what place was that? But of course, his father must have been the one with the camera.

When he did find a photograph with his father on it (the four-year-old Graham scowling with a bucket on one of their seaside holidays, his father in the background crouched over an elaborate sand fortress) he had a sudden memory of the occasion and a shock of revelation.

That fortress! The fetching of water to moisten the sand, the endless cutting of sharp edges with the spade which his father had taken from him, his father's absorption in the extended walls and slopes down which a tennis ball was expected to roll. Graham had been tired, bored and excluded, and at one point had accidentally spoilt some precariously-assembled feature. His father had hit him then, in a quite unjustifiable temper. Graham saw it all clearly. His father had not been put upon at all. He was not deferent, not side-lined. He had been feared. He was always hitting his son for almost no reason at all, and over the years Graham had persuaded himself to forget it. Had he hit his wife as well? Or did he just hit his son? Not beatings, nothing like that, but flashes of rage, cuffs round the ears.

Graham was reminded, in a flood of self-pity, how in fact his whole life had been a protracted escape from the emotional constraints of his childhood, the uncertainties, the wish to please. But now he wondered at the motives of those who had brought him into the world. They must have loved him, must have wanted him, as he loved Susan and Michael. Was it his mother, after all, who was weak? Had he simply never lived up to his father's expectations? He remembered the year when he graduated and his fellow finalists were feasted by their families. His own parents had contrived yet again to be in Lanzarote.

He hadn't made that mistake himself. He had always been there for his children, and Maddie had been a rock in that respect. Susan and Michael had every reason to be grateful. Didn't they?

The boxes went back into the attic, and his reflections similarly went back into the unlit recesses of his mind. Blood pressure 178/72.

The blood pressure readings had been very up and down. Some of them he took several times before he obtained what he felt were acceptable figures, something within the parameters of reasonable health. He didn't think of this as cheating. It more or less said you could do it in the leaflet that came with the monitor. But he wouldn't go out of his way to say so to Dr Driffield.

When he did return to the surgery, Dr Driffield ("Paul!") proposed to put him on statins, and sent him through to the nurse for his ECG.

"We'll get a better picture in due course," he said. "But your stats are reasonably OK. I'd like a better figure for the cholesterol and the liver function."

Graham was tempted to say: "I'm not an old man", but remembered that he had said that on his previous visit. Instead he said:

"I'm not overweight."

Dr Driffield laughed.

"Well, yes, as a matter of fact you are."

His height had been measured, and he had been weighed, on arrival.

"Your BMI is well over 30."

Graham couldn't see how the calculation could be accurate. He was weighed with most of his clothes on. He had keys and heavy change in his pockets. He said as much.

"We make allowance for that," said Dr Driffield.

He thought that his doctor was becoming rather short with him. Was it because he was beginning to think him too cavalier about his life-style? Graham had been very defensive about his weekly units of alcohol, saying with a laugh that no establishment in Oxford served wine in 115ml measures. Or was it that he refused to call him Paul? In fact, he was studiously not calling him anything at all, which seemed in a way just as friendly as calling him by his first name. Perhaps that seemed to indicate a lack of respect. But it was no reason to treat him as Graham imagined he must have to treat most of his other patients, who were all obese, addicted to junk foods and drinking far too much.

"I do have a large frame, you know," he objected. "I used to play quite a bit of Rugby."

"Not so much now, I suppose," smiled Dr Driffield.

"A spot of golf," said Graham.

"Yes, of course,"

It was the only acknowledgement of their shared social status and it amounted to very little, Graham thought. And it was just as well, wasn't it? He thought of ordering drinks at the Club with Driffield looking over his shoulder, and felt that nothing could be more uncomfortable.

Well that was that. He was now on medication. The first sign that he was an old man, after all. He thought of hypertension as an oddly misnamed condition. He wasn't tense. He just felt jittery sometimes. And wasn't "tension" a little different after all from tenseness? Wasn't tension a productive state of things? Tension was the tautness of the bow before the arrow is loosened. A gathering of power. Maddie's cello strings had to be screwed to the right tension before a note could be played. The opposite of tense was lax, and Graham hated laxness in all its forms. Or was the word laxity? That sounded like a condition of the bowels that nobody could possibly want.

By the time he got home, he had put it all from his mind. He even left his prescription unopened in its paper bag on the kitchen table. He took the ring of garden keys down from their hook (these now included not only the keys of the pod and the garden gate, but also the key to Maddie's chest of drawers) and went out at the back. He had been neglecting the garden since Maddie's death. The roses were unpruned and the hedges untrimmed. But the insects didn't care. They knew nothing of his state of mind. The bees entered and retreated from the lavender busily like shoppers at the supermarket shelves. Orange butterflies crossed the lawn at shoulder height as though somehow knocked from side to side in the still air.

Graham, too, was busy in his own way, busy with his grief. He was going to open Maddie's little chest of drawers at last, and he was stirring himself, like an actor about to go on stage, to rise appropriately to the occasion. He had felt the same way when clearing the wardrobe and laying out Maddie's clothes on the bed. These were the veritable signs and appearances of her being of this world, the familiar forms of her recognizability. Their hollowness, their fragility and limpness, was devastating to him. But he knew he had played his part well. He had offered them to her friends as trophies, which he felt was both magnanimous and economical, both sentimental and practical. There was nothing in it that he might be accused of. He had been shocked and upset that his offers had been largely declined.

He had put off this further moment of recognition and understanding, and without yet knowing what he would find, he unlocked the drawer, was already weeping.

He had expected letters in the drawer. Perhaps even, he thought with a sudden lurch of hatred, some secret adulterous letters. He knew that he had no reason to believe that such letters or the hidden affairs that they would represent might exist, but it pleased his mood to fear it. There were no letters, but a locket and chain that was familiar to him from their early days, a note-book half-bound in leather and marbled paper, and one or two other bits and pieces. He took everything back to the kitchen and spread it on the table.

He felt as though Maddie had invisibly entered the room.

He opened the notebook at the beginning. There was an elegant drawing of a snake with a patterned skin, its head curved round and staring at the reader with popping eyes. And the written text that followed began:

"This is the Chinese Year of the Snake. It's also the year of the prick, and the Chinese Position."

Graham paused to take stock of this. He was shocked at the language. He had no idea which Chinese years were which, though he knew that they came around in cycles. The handwriting was Maddie's, at least a version of it which he recognised, but dating back a long time ago, surely. He glanced down the page. Though he recognised the handwriting, the sentiments and attitudes he didn't think he recognised, quite. If they were Maddie's, they seemed alien to him. What was it? They didn't seem to include him. They belonged to a young Maddie, to Maddie before he knew her. Or was that quite true? There were things written that struck a bell. It was a diary of sorts, was it? There were no dates. The entries, if they could be called entries, simply followed one after the other.

He read on. It was even rather like a sort of story:

42

"This is the Chinese Year of the Snake. It's also the year of the prick, and the Chinese position.

To Caro's in Pimlico. Stuccoed Primlico. Knock me down, but she's got a man! Several men, actually, because there are such a lot of them about. I didn't know she had it in her. To coin a phrase.

Maddie, meet W, but you can't have him. Maddie, meet T, if you can bear to. Maddie, meet G, ha-ha-ha.

Don't tell, Maddie. Don't tell.

Who could tell?

Introductions aren't always followed by Allegros.

Lunch with G. Oh, the Roast Beef of Old England! I don't think I've ever been walked along the King's Road before held by the elbow. A charmer.

Caro says that G is obviously besotted with me. What a strange word that is, besotted. Besotted. I was besotted all by myself on the sofa. I must really get besotted with someone else.

D at the GH for cherry soup and blinis. He said that Schumann had a brain the size of a walnut. What could he mean? The next day he stopped in the middle of the Adagio and was simply weeping. I don't know if it is all just put on, or if he can't help it. It wasn't the music I don't think. Three minutes in the ring with G would be the end of him.

Caro says W is a monster for touching her up in a taxi, but it's obvious that she didn't mind. She also says that G is really a great big pussy-cat behind it all. You could have fooled me. Little does she know! Pussy-cats have claws! Mind what you say or it'll come back at you when you'd forgotten all about it. That large red face and the invisible eyebrows. His habit of jutting his lip out when he is thinking. His hair, too. He'll be bald when he's 30. But he makes the back of my neck prickle.

I think G is actually frightened of Caro. D certainly is.

Caro says that D played the virginals at college. I can believe it. No more Schumann. Rachmaninov recommended.

Waiting for D to move is like waiting for the rush-hour bus in the Marylebone Road, full of anxiety and uncomfortable when it arrives. When G makes his move, you know where you are immediately. Sex by numbers. Rough stuff, too.

Not bad, not bad at all. Showed him off to Dilys.

When the exams are over, I'll make my mind up then. I might even ask God.

He's taken me to the races. The races! Five pounds each way on Eternal Bliss. But he still doesn't like to lose an argument. A short fuse. A short fuse and then a rather pointless little boom.

The body makes the mind up for it. The body makes up for the mind. The mind makes up to the body. And then it's too late.

The Priory in October, without the tribe. Or will they all be there? The Selection Committee. Daddy looking down his nose.

That lovely Gershwin song: 'Where *you* go *I* go, 'cause *I* gotta *go* where *you* go!' All or nothing.

Help, help, help. God is a bit cross.

The scarlet soldiers are coming, my dear, down in the valley. What a relief. Nothing. Nothing will come of nothing.

The Priory a success, more or less. Daddy likes someone who knows where he's going and knows less than he does about Buxtehude. And plays bridge. Hooray! Has it only been five months?"

And so it went on, with more little drawings and a comic account of their wedding, sometimes excited, sometimes wise, sometimes comprehensible, often less so. Graham could remember Maddie's circle, and a few of her old friends, but some of the initials defeated him. D was Dan, wasn't he, that utter wet creep who ended up in the Doncaster Symphonia or something? Graham had seen him off all right. He now thought that all this must have been written in 1989.

The diary seemed to modulate into anxieties about the niceties of her playing, and then there were notes about babies, how she didn't want to have babies, how perhaps it might be good to have babies, what it might actually be like to have babies, then what her babies were like, lists of things, and many gnomic thoughts.

This was Maddie right enough, but Maddie pure and young, or not very pure but very young, facing the world, with life reduced to the words she could control, and to the essence of the things she cared about. And it was also of course the beautiful Maddie of the little nose and curling lip, who could always make men weep.

He blotted his eyes, and leafed forward in the notebook, looking for mentions of himself.

Did he not know in his heart what she thought of him, all their troubles, the very unfair bad times with her, the things that Susan and Michael would never know? No, he didn't really know any more. He had put them from him, like food on a plate that he couldn't eat, and once they were binned they were forgotten.

He smiled fondly to think that she, too, in the delicacy of her sensibility might have forgotten them. But if that were the case he would appear in these pages as his better self, the forgiven husband, the just and reasonable father. His strictness, his temper, his sarcasm, his violence, these would be understood and redeemed here in these busy thoughtful pages, just as she would confess her own weaknesses. He spent the better part of an hour fingering the pages backwards and forwards looking for his name.

There was no further mention of him at all.

I t wasn't until the morning of the Association party that Marian next door reminded him of it. She was getting on her bicycle to go and buy some smoked salmon. Everyone was supposed to bring something.

How could he have forgotten? He had had his jars of olives and packets of cheese twists in the larder for weeks, bought early precisely so that he shouldn't forget. It was in his diary, but unless he remembered to look in his diary how would he know that it was there? These lapses of memory were disconcerting, but he was soon overtaken by another worry. Was his contribution enough? Should he have made something? Ann Sims always made a lemon drizzle cake, and if the weather was really promising Colin Sherwood would let it be known that if someone undertook to bring sausages he would fire up his barbecue.

The party usually took place in the Sherwoods' garden because there was a friendly gate between them and Lottie Lubeck's house next door, much overgrown with honeysuckle but not above being wrenched open for people to pass from no. 3 to no. 2 in a carefree al fresco spirit, drinks in hand. But Lottie was away for the summer and it was thought better to hold the party elsewhere. Phyl had offered her garden at their annual meeting: "It's enormous. Don't you remember, we used to hold the party there ages ago. Lots of room. Perhaps someone might mow it for me?" Colin had said to Bill afterwards that something more like a scythe might be necessary, but between them they had managed to tidy up a major part of it in good time for the party. Colin had little enthusiasm for doing it. He thought that providing his barbecue was quite enough.

However early one arrived for the Association party, Father Eustace was always there first. The children came early, too, in order to seize buns and crisps and set up shops and schools in the bushes. Graham disliked his neighbours' children on the whole, the new ones from no. 9 whose names he could never remember, the Terry brood, the Sherwood girl who was now nearly grown up but could be quite as silly and irritating as the rest of them. He wouldn't have put it past her to have done something foolish with that syringe he had found, and infect herself. It would be her own fault. Susan and Michael would never have chalked obscenities on the pavements when they were young. It really brought down the tone of the place.

He thought of saying as much to Father Eustace, who he found beaming beneath an old pear tree, but decided not to because the last time they had spoken he had pretended to be concerned for the children's welfare if they were to come across syringes and he would appear to be illogical. Really, he was more concerned with general propriety and the reputation of the neighbourhood. That was important as well, surely, and it maintained house prices. He didn't think that some of his neighbours cared at all about it.

He added his own contributions to the trestle table incongruously covered with dishes of cheese, bottles of lemonade, Pringles, smoked salmon on rye-bread, iced buns, waxed paper bowls of halved strawberries with piped aerosol cream on top, and peanuts. He poured himself a glass of Lirac, which was the best he could find there, as yet unopened. His own bottle, a supermarket Riesling, he hid behind the other anonymous Pinot Grigios and Sauvignons.

46

"We enjoyed your sermon on Sunday," he said, raising his glass in a familiar and friendly way to Father Eustace, who though formally in his soutane, could always be treated in a neighbourly way. He might in just the same tone of voice have said: "Your geraniums are looking good at the moment."

Father Eustace's little shrug of demurral might have been intended to suggest that just as geraniums have their own way of growing according to the conditions of nature, so the very Word of God had nothing very much to do with him.

What could he say next? Graham always felt a bit stiff on these contrived social occasions. He nervously looked around for Effie, and was relieved to see that Father Eustace's dog was not there.

"Michael asked afterwards why Jesus was described as a thief," he blurted out. But he hadn't meant to say that at all.

"Ah," replied Father Eustace, looking deeply into his already almost empty glass. He seemed quite unprepared for a theological discussion.

"I mean," said Graham, "I could see of course that that obviously wasn't what was being said. It was a strange thing for Michael to say."

"Quite so," said Father Eustace. "It wouldn't be very sensible, would it? No, it's just a parable. A metaphor, really. You have to be vigilant, ready to admit Christ. Ready, I suppose, for death."

"But not as a thief," said Graham, persisting.

"Not as a thief exactly," agreed Father Eustace. "Though death could be regarded as a thief. Theft of the body, though not of the soul, which Satan of course desires. Have you read any Middle English? Perhaps not? They loved allegory then, you know, the body as a castle, the soul as its treasure, the vices as the thief who must not be admitted, all that sort of thing. *Sawles Warde*, Wit and Will, Reason the lord of the castle, his wife the betraying appetite? Like the drunken servant in Matthew?"

Graham gazed at him in stupefied and smiling incomprehension at this babble. The betraying appetite of a wife caught his passing attention, but he was sure that Father Eustace knew nothing at all about wives.

"Look," said Father Eustace. "Very good question, actually, but I think I must go and fill up my glass."

Graham was relieved in a way. The man doesn't really know what he's talking about, he thought. And he can't answer the question. Like a bloody politician.

He turned in an aimless half-circle to see who he might talk to. The garden was filling up. He exchanged a few words with Phyl and Ann Sims's sister, before being button-holed by Bill Peacock.

"Haven't seen much of you since that presentation, old boy," said Bill. "Bit of a large ask, don't you think?"

Graham thought for a moment that he had said "large arse", which would in a way have perfectly described Con Bullett.

"It looked quite promising to me," said Graham.

"Did it?" asked Bill. "When I told Marian about it, she said we shouldn't touch it with a barge-pole."

"Ah," said Graham, noncommittally. He might have been referring to Marian's expected wisdom in such matters, or to the fact that he himself was now entirely unencumbered by such wifely caution, and that in either case he was consumed with pity for Bill's predicament. "What are you going to do?"

"Going to do?" said Bill. "I'm not going to do anything. Do I look as though I have piles of spare cash lying about? I'm still trying to keep my mother in the care home."

"Of course," agreed Graham.

"Without selling her house, that is," said Bill. "I mean, I might have managed a small amount, say 200 shares. Just for fun, you know. Because that's all it is."

"Fun?"

"It's just a gamble, isn't it? He can't promise us that the shares will go up when he goes public. And they might go down again before we can sell them, mightn't they? Wasn't there a clause about waiting? And surely they'll go down in any case if we are all selling them. Do you know anything about new issues? I thought not. Nor do I."

Bill looked truculent in his argument, as though he expected Graham to persuade him otherwise. But Graham couldn't summon the energy to contradict him. He hadn't really focussed on all these details and possibilities anyway. He thought that Bill's attitude was feeble, and that it was feeble because Marian led him by the nose. Graham wouldn't have let Maddie dictate to him on an important matter like this.

Colin's barbecue was beginning to smell, and people were backing away from the smoke. The children were all laughing and shouting, and Graham thought that it was because they had come running back for sausages, but Dick Terry said it was because they had found something exciting in the garden.

Bill went to get Phyl, and a group of them all followed Dick and his oldest daughter Sharon, prancing theatrically in orange shorts and a pastel-coloured flowered top, up to the end of Phyl's garden. A path had been mown up the middle, beyond the main gathering of the party, dividing into two when it encountered an old lime tree with the remains of a bench that had once been constructed around it, but then petering out rather than meeting up again. They passed the collapsed frame of a greenhouse, and had to bend beneath an apple tree before reaching the overgrown end of the garden, where tiers of bramble and ivy climbed into the branches of the perimeter trees, some holly and an old ash that was actually in Graham's garden.

That was the strange thing about these gardens. You might have thought, when you were in the Close itself, that all the gardens fanned out behind the houses in more or less equal size. But Phyl's long garden at no. 1, reaching away from her house in what was effectively an L-shape, constrained the size of the gardens of her immediate neighbours, Lottie at no. 2 and the Sherwoods at no. 3, and that might have been one of the reasons why the Sherwoods and Lottie's predecessor had arranged the friendly gate between them, a rather odd thing between neighbours, but there had been a reason for it. Graham's garden was much longer, and the left-hand corner of it abutted on Phyl's garden and the outside lane. Now that they had reached the tangled end of things, Graham was very close to his own property. He could actually see the roof of the pod with its strangely sprouting vegetation.

But their attention was now focussed on what the children had found. Half-hidden in the bushes was a small flattish tent, with four seams meeting at the centre like a cardinal's hat. It was worn and stained, but professional-looking, like something you might see at the foot of the Himalayas, a grinning climber standing in front of it with a frosty and icicled beard.

"Look!" said Sharon proudly, as though she might have put it up herself. And before anyone could stop her she had crawled inside. The little ones hung back.

"What *are* you doing, for God's sake," shouted Dick, reaching for her ankle and missing it. "You don't know what's in there."

"It's all right", said Sharon's voice. "I've already been inside. There's nobody here."

"It's not yours, is it, Phyl?" said Colin. "I didn't notice it when we were mowing."

"Never seen it in my life," said Phyl.

The other children were squealing with excitement now, and wanted to crawl inside themselves.

"That's quite enough," shouted Graham. "All of you, out of there!"

Colin looked at him sharply. It wasn't Graham's place to tell his daughter what she could or couldn't do, and Graham's reputation for telling the children off in the street had been more than once discussed by his neighbours. Still, nobody disagreed with his sentiments on this occasion.

When Sharon finally emerged, she had her arms full. There was a knapsack, a torch, some books and papers, and a bottle.

"There's a box of black bananas in there," she said triumphantly. "And a duvet. Yuck!"

"Yuck! Yuck! Yuck!" cried the other children, capering about.

"It looks like someone's camping," said Bill. "How did they get in?"

"Not difficult," said Colin. "Look at the state of the fence."

The fence was leaning inwards but also broken and splayed outwards at the same time under the weight of branches and clumps of ivy. And it seemed to have been moved recently, showing splinters. And with a lurch of anxiety Graham saw that the length of fence between Phyl's garden and his own was in a similar state of disrepair, not noticeable from his side because of his old bay tree. Were all the gardens as neglected as this? Did the houses boast cropped lawns, shining windows and azaleas at the front like bright faces to meet the day, while hidden away at the back were the secret places of shame?

Graham had taken charge of the books and papers from Sharon and was turning them over. One of them was some sort of textbook, with graphs and statistics. Another was *The House at Pooh Corner.*

"Let me see," said Phyl. "Oh, how extraordinary! This encampment looks a bit like the house at Pooh Corner itself." She didn't seem at all disturbed by this intrusion into her property.

"Not a child, though, is it?" said Bill.

Graham was looking now at the papers, folded A4 sheets, scribbled all over with tiny writing. He was utterly amazed to see a photograph of himself.

It stared back at him greyly and indistinctly, with the nervous ingratiating expression that faces assume when being inspected. The fact that he was now inspecting it himself seemed to him quite incomprehensible. It was as mystifying as the climax of a conjuring trick. It was as though Colin or Bill had set it all up.

It was the copy of his passport that he had scanned on his printer, the metallic colours and iridescent security printing reduced to dull speckled uniformity, but his official likeness perfectly recognisable.

These were his papers. They should have been in the hall ready to be taken to the building society, and here they were in a filthy tent in Phyl's filthy garden. They must have been stolen by that young tramp, the dosser, the homeless squatter who'd been hanging around for ages and had had the cheek to come to his house to borrow a pen. To borrow a pen? What a fantasy! To be *given* a pen (quite a good one, he remembered, one of those fine-line Pilots) and then to steal from his hallway, when his back was turned. What else might he have taken? Or from Phyl, when she filled his water bottle?

"These are actually mine, would you believe it," he said, thrusting the papers into an inside pocket. He didn't want anyone to see them, or to know anything about his private affairs. "We have a thief among us."

"Goodness," said Phyl. "Where did you lose them?"

"I didn't lose them," said Graham. "They were stolen from me, obviously. By your friend I gave that pen to."

"Not my friend, Graham," said Phyl sharply.

"That's not good, is it?" said Bill. "We'll have to do something about this."

"What are they?" asked Phyl.

Graham didn't want to say exactly what the papers were, and felt that in being vague about his explanation he was somehow making it seem unimportant.

"Well, you've got them back now," said Phyl. "Since he needed a pen I expect he wanted some spare paper to write on."

"You can buy pens and notebooks for almost nothing practically anywhere," said Graham.

"Not if you don't have the money," replied Phyl.

"I think I should go to the police," said Bill. As the convenor and treasurer of the Close Association he was always ready to take on such responsibility.

"I wish you luck," said Graham bitterly. "They don't want to know." He told them about the syringe, and his fruitless phone call.

"We don't actually know that the syringe has any connection with the tent," said Phyl. "And all this is quite touching, isn't it? Winnie-the-Pooh! It might all belong to a child, anyway. We should put everything back. Come on, Sharon. Let's put these things back."

Graham was amazed.

"Why don't we roll it all up and take it to the dump?"

"Good idea," said Bill.

"No," said Phyl. "I don't think so. It wouldn't be quite fair. Let's leave it and go back to the party."

Phyl had her way. The men reluctantly respected her authority, not least as a woman of social conscience and tender feelings. And her house was worth so much more than theirs. That was always some sort of unacknowledged difference between them.

Graham was furious. It was not only an invasion of property and privacy, with a gross personal inconvenience to himself. It was a sign of the collapse of the social order, with no one taking on any responsibility for anything, and people like Phyl, from a

52

very privileged family, after all, were as much to blame as the feckless street dwellers who felt that the world owed them a living, and that they could do as they liked.

When he finally left the party, he had decided that Phyl's views were quite hopeless. The headline in the day's *Guardian* lying on her hall table seemed to bear him out ("Tories in Disarray") and he almost laughed when he noticed that her carriage clock was once more showing 2.20. Stuck in the past, he thought, like its owner, and the political party he knew she supported.

But he didn't laugh when he got home and smoothed out the purloined papers, for the crucial one, the original notification from his building society of the details of the controversial saver account was not among them. Nor was it in the hall where he had left everything. Where was it?

And it was only at this moment, back at the kitchen table where he had been re-reading Maddie's diary, that he was again assailed with a sense of the emptiness of his life. If he did not appear as a husband and father in those pages, where did he, could he, so appear? It was as though he hadn't existed at all. Even Schumann had a greater presence there than he did. Did Schumann ever lose things, he wondered, the mad bastard?

D espite having had several glasses of wine at the party, and red wine at that, Graham felt that he needed a drink. He poured himself a scotch, and put two slices of bread in the toaster. He would have to search the house for the account details, since he must have left them somewhere else. Or wait, no. The thief must have taken them all but left only some of them, the ones with plenty of blank space that he could write on, in his tent. He could still have the really important one on him, or perhaps have thrown it away.

He was going to fry a couple of eggs, no, three eggs, and smother the lot in tomato ketchup. He couldn't be bothered with anything more than that. Besides, he had eaten four blackened sausages from the barbecue, and a lot of nuts. He didn't see why he should cook for himself, and didn't much anymore. He didn't really feel that he could cook at all. That meal for Michael and Koon-Mi had been ridiculous.

Now he was probably not only going to be too late in transferring money to his current account to pay for his Bullettpod shares, but might actually have difficulty in proving that he had the account at all. The building society must have a record of it somewhere. But suppose in the process of digitisation and putting everything on-line his account (and perhaps other older long-standing accounts) had been left out. He could well imagine such a mistake, a bored clerk typing in lists. Interest was set to accumulate and be re-invested, so he would only have had annual statements. But where were those? He had found no recent ones, and had never thought to check and discover that they were missing at the time. Perhaps the account had in some way disappeared years ago, and in carelessness he had never noticed. In the long term he imagined it must be recoverable, but it now looked as though he wasn't going to be able to buy those shares. It was already the 26th of June!

As he sat at the kitchen table, angrily shovelling in the eggs, he looked at the writing on the sheet that contained the reproduction of his passport. The double-spread of the passport took up only half a page. The added writing began at right angles to it in the blank half of the page, and continued overleaf. The writing was neat and regular, which surprised him. It had a confident flow, with triangulated loops to some of the letters, and tiny circles instead of dots over each "i". There were only a few words crossed out here and there, so that it was clear to see that what was written out in short lines was a kind of fair copy of something, a series of statements, with larger gaps between some of the lines than others:

When a wife leaves she leaves
her husband alone
when a mother leaves she also leaves
a part of her self in her son
apart

i have held a hand that was
once held out to me
but it was not her hand

i have given you enough of my self
to see in your eyes
a reflexion of my incompleteness

mother of mine you
kept me out of harm and
kept me for your self
now you have gone
i can only keep to my self

i travelled the world over
deserts and seas to find you
only to realise that you had
gone nowhere only
away from your self

when they say i have failed
they are so wrong
i cant have failed until
i have tried

Graham soon decided that these were meant to be poems. He knew enough about modern poetry to realise that if you didn't capitalise the personal pronoun and didn't use any punctuation you had a peculiar and exaggerated idea of your own significance and a dismissive attitude to your readers. This accorded very well with his understanding of modern poetry and of the character of the young man who had written the poems, who he now began to think of as "the dosser." He liked the word because it also sounded like "tosser", so that the thief was not only homeless and taking advantage of other people's property, but was a pretentious failure as well.

And he once again resented seeing his own innocent normal face (the face that after all represented him to the officials of foreign countries in a legal document also validating his citizenship) associated unknowingly with all this drivel. It was an appropriation worse in its way than the dosser having pitched his filthy tent in Phyl's garden. How could he have the effrontery to be living there? He could have no access to a lavatory. Graham dreaded to think what else might lie hidden in the bushes. And what about the girl he had seen? Why were there two of them? The tent hadn't seemed big enough for two. Perhaps she didn't sleep there as well. Perhaps they had quarrelled. The voices he had heard in the lane that day had seemed to be arguing, querulous and inconsiderate.

Graham put his plate in the sink and went into the living-room to watch *Britain's Got Talent*. Although he was no longer taking his blood pressure, and the monitor had been returned to the surgery, he knew that if he had taken it, it would have hit the roof.

Alone in the wide bed where he had once been accustomed to exerting his physical charms to heal the quarrels and divisions of the day, Graham woke to a distant strangulated cry that he had often heard in recent weeks. He didn't think it had actually woken him, as sometimes happened with Ann Sims's Jack Russell, yapping vigorously and far too early, presumably when Ann got up to make herself a cup of tea. But it was persistent and annoying. And it came from not far away, too near at any rate to be a bird from one of the Marston farms. Someone was keeping a cockerel in their suburban garden! Surely there were regulations about that? A limitation on livestock in properties designated as dwellings?

He would find out, and write to the Council. Perhaps it wasn't a farmyard bird at all. Perhaps one of the effete schoolmasters at that posh prep school had acquired a peacock to entertain the boys. But he didn't think it sounded like a peacock.

Maddie's notebook was still out on the kitchen table where he had left it. He felt once again as though she were there, and had come down to breakfast before him. Yes, as though she had come down before him and wasn't speaking to him. How weird. He hadn't prepared himself for this. He shrugged to himself, and after he had eaten something he left for work, to push files around his desk all day. Not much more of this, he thought. I shall retire before long and begin a new life. I'll move nearer to Susan and the boys. I'll buy a sports car and go to the races again.

But the sports car he had in mind (a white Nissan 370Z Nismo: he looked it up again online when he was in the office) would be out of his reach if he was going to be too late to make some fast money in Bullettpods. It cost just under £40K and so escaped the ridiculous extra annual VED charge of £310 a year. Graham, had carefully worked it all out. With a little help from his current account and credit card he might have been able to buy as many as ten tranches of shares, and that if what Con had been promising was true he might easily end up with over £60K, a clear profit of £25K. Graham knew he should be realistic, but that Nissan would be his with something over to reinvest properly. If only he could complete that transfer from his building society in time.

When he got home he tried to make a systematic search, but his motivation gradually weakened. He felt sure that he had left everything in the hall, and that the dosser had taken the lot. What use was it to go back to his filing cabinet? He had only recently collected everything needed from there. He wouldn't have put the papers back. Could he have taken them to the pod? No, of course not. The dosser had some of them and had been scribbling on them. He must have all of them then. They had all been together.

Still, he would go back to the pod. Now that he had found Maddie's notebook the business of clearing it completely could begin. The last relic of the shrine had been removed, the sole worshipper implicitly rebuked and ignored: the pod could now be re-established as a secular space. He thought he might have water piped out there and a sink plumbed in. He could brew his own beer there. He would reclaim it as a man-space and show it off to his friends.

But when he went to the hook in the kitchen, the keys were not there.

At first, he thought that they must have been left on the kitchen table. Or on some convenient surface when he had returned from the pod the previous evening, his hands full of Maddie's things, which he feared dropping. But no. Could the dosser have broken into the house in his absence and taken them? Surely not. No sign of a break-in.

Not in his pocket? No. Another pocket? What had he been wearing?

It didn't take him long to realise that he must have left the keys in the door of the pod. He almost ran to the back door and hastened down the garden path. How foolish! One of these days he might go to work and find that he'd left the front door unlocked, and anyone could walk in. Maddie had always been very careful, and between them he thought they had kept a tight ship. Ann Sims had been burgled a few years back, and that was why she had bought her dog. They were a Neighbourhood Watch Area, and Bill Peacock kept them all informed of any problems. Nowhere was impregnable these days.

Yes, the pod door was open. What an idiot he was. But as he came nearer he saw that there were no keys hanging from the lock.

When he went into the pod he found the dosser inside, seated on the floor with his back to the rear wall. Light from the Velux in the flat roof faintly illuminated the grey cowl of his hood and the tops of his wrists resting on his raised knees. A moth had got in and was fluttering about the ceiling. The boy's posture against the wall was uncannily like that of the homeless men that Graham was used to seeing in the city streets, but self-absorbed rather than resigned, wistful rather than abject. And he looked very pale and ill.

Graham was conscious of a feeling, unrecognised until this moment, that he had for a long time known that they would meet again. He suddenly saw that it was part of his destiny to confront the dosser deep in his own territory. But he was enraged at it. The dosser was not only a failure in life, evidently, but a thief as well.

"Out," said Graham decisively. "Out you go!"

The boy looked up at him wearily, with no apparent intention of moving.

"Oh, it's you," he said. "I see you've got another little house here."

"It's not a house," said Graham scornfully. "It's a pod."

"Oh," said the boy. "A pod? Isn't that what those cages are called at the Mexican border? Where Trump imprisons all the immigrants?"

"It's a pod," repeated Graham uselessly. Why was he getting into an argument with this intruder? Why was the intruder even talking to him? He should be bundling him out straight away. But he realised, as he looked around for them and couldn't see them, on the chest or anywhere else, that the dosser must have the keys on him. And that he would have to get them off him first.

"Who do you keep shut up here, then?" the boy asked. And he laughed, coughing deeply, as if to recognise the absurdity of his question. He seemed not at all put out to be discovered there. "Pod no. 1 Pod no. 2. You know."

"How did you get in here?" asked Graham.

"It wasn't locked," said the boy. "It wasn't even shut."

"Give me the keys," said Graham. "You've got the keys. And those papers of mine."

The boy kicked out his legs so that they were flat against the floor. He was very thin. His arms rested against his legs now. He looked like a marionette.

He ignored Graham's request.

"We could live here, you know," he coughed. "Big enough for two."

He spoke without enthusiasm, as though reluctantly agreeing with an over-eager estate agent. Then he looked Graham directly in the eye.

"Was it you who trashed my bivouac?"

"Your bivouac?" Graham repeated the word with infinite disgust. "You think you're on some nice little camping holiday, do you? God almighty."

"You did, then," said the boy. "And you took my poems."

"I took your poems? "said Graham. '*You* took my papers! You scribbled all over my passport."

"Your passport?' said the boy, puzzled.

"The copy of my passport."

"Oh."

The boy considered this for a moment, and then surprisingly sneezed, so that a stalactite of slightly bloody mucus was left hanging from his nose. He made no effort to wipe it away. Graham turned from it in disgust.

"You took my papers," he repeated. "You stole my papers when I went to get you that pen."

"Oh, the pen," said the boy. "Yes, I came to give you back the pen." And he fumbled inside his jerkin as if to find it, without success.

"You're a liar," said Graham. "A thief and a liar, and you're trespassing."

"So you did trash my bivouac," said the boy sadly, and the odd phrase now began to take on the strange formality of some arcane legal transgression.

At the back of his mind Graham was wondering if Bill Peacock had in fact got rid of that wretched tent and its pathetic contents after all. Phyl had said to leave it, but knowing Bill he wouldn't have put it past him to have already bundled it all up, and perhaps gone to the police, as he had threatened.

"I didn't steal your papers," said the boy. He was staring at the floor. "I did take some paper from a blue bin. That's all right, isn't it? Recycling. I find lots in the recycling."

Graham was stung by this. The dosser was bringing back the pen, was he? Graham had himself left the pod key in its lock, had he? And been instrumental perhaps in the displacement of the dosser's ridiculous tent? And certainly in removing the sheet with those idiot poems? And what's more, thrown away all his own crucial papers by taking them out to the blue bin with a pile of newspapers? All this was his own fault then, was it?

He was losing it, was he?

Oh no, he wasn't to be blamed for this. He wasn't going to be blamed for losing the chance to make some easy thousands. He wasn't going to be blamed for this invasion of his sacred space. He wasn't going to be blamed for the current boredom of his life, and the sense of having become only a cipher in the middle of it. What might they be saying about him? "Poor Graham, he's really going to pieces. We must do something about Graham."

Well, "poor Graham" could look after himself, thank you very much. He reached down and grabbed the boy by the shoulders.

"Up you get," he shouted. "Up!"

The boy made no attempt to get up, and from that angle Graham couldn't raise him. As he pulled, so the boy simply slid sideways in a sitting position, looking up at him as though it were some kind of game. Indeed, he raised his arms to grasp Graham's, and looked at him questioningly. Graham was reminded of times when Michael was little and he had swung him round and round above the lawn, clasping his wrists. Such requested horseplay had usually come too late in the afternoon, when everyone was tired, and it had usually ended in tears.

The keys had fallen on the floor beside him, whether out of a pocket or from his lap wasn't clear. The boy let go of Graham's left arm and reached for the keys.

"No you don't, you little shit," said Graham as he stamped on the boy's wrist to stop him getting them. He reached down to pick them up himself, and as he did so put more of his weight on that foot. There was an audible crack.

Graham had the keys in his hand. The boy's other arm was flailing about, pulling at his trousers. His gasp of pain had turned into a quiet wail. He was grasping Graham's leg now, as if to pull himself up.

"You're a fucking sadist," he said. There was nothing to the boy, a thin chest and angular uncoordinated limbs, trying to turn on his side so that he could get up, his clothes loose on him like a scarecrow. And he couldn't get up because he couldn't use the arm with the broken wrist.

Graham had never felt such contempt for anyone before. He tried to shake his leg free, and kicked out, catching the boy's now raised knees.

"You like doing that, don't you?" said the boy. And despite his pain he was almost smiling up at Graham, as though in pity. "You enjoy kicking someone?"

"Oh yes," said Graham, decidedly, suddenly finding himself on the dangerous threshold of a rage that somehow, deliciously, he need no longer forbid himself from crossing. It was like a door that had swung open in his head, revealing the limitless possibility of punishing this transgression. Who could now prevent him from doing so? There was no longer any voice to tell him to hold back. "Oh yes, I do. I do."

He freed his leg, drew it back and kicked.

"You filthy, filthy little squirt," he hissed, as he kicked again, and again, and again, holding his retrieved pod keys above his head like a prize at a children's party, where all the other children were to be humiliated by not winning.

The boy moaned, his knees drawn up towards his chin, across which travelled a small trail of blood.

"You're a liar and a thief," shouted Graham, as his shoe met bone. And then something softer. He went on kicking. And kicking. And kicking.

G raham's head was thudding violently, and a circular mist seemed to be revolving in front of his eyes in contrary directions at the same time. He had had this before, and then thought it was something like a migraine. But this felt bad. Without quite knowing what he was doing, he managed to lock the pod door behind him and get down the path into the house, where he was immediately sick in the downstairs loo.

He had no rational thoughts about what had just occurred, but he was aware that he had lost control of himself. He felt that he had been threatened, but couldn't have explained to anyone in what way, or for what purpose. He had responded to a threatening situation, that was all. But look what it had turned into! His mind was quite blank as to the justice of his response, or about the degree of outrage he had felt, or about the effect of what he had done. But what had happened thrust out of consideration all other aspects of his life. He couldn't remember whatever else he might have been going to do before he went to the pod, or think of what he might do now. He couldn't for the moment imagine what might be the consequences of what he had done. Indeed, his entire future life had now no meaning.

A voice inside his head, putting all this helpfully to one side, told him that he was ill. This realisation that he was in a state needing medical attention now occupied him totally, and he concentrated his mind on the business of seeking some help in the matter.

Could he speak? Could he find his mobile? The landline receiver in the hall made no sense to him. It might just as well have been a piece of modernist sculpture or a tiny alien spacecraft. He had no idea where his mobile might be. His dizziness became, not an internal condition of bodily balance, but an external force pushing relentlessly at his head from both sides at once.

How did he manage to get out of his front door and across his front lawn? Did he know where he was going? Who was he hoping to find? Would anyone in the Close be outside at that time? Anyone? Even a child playing, who would see what a state he was in?

He knelt on the grass, and was conscious of putting out his hands, nothing much beyond that. Whoever saw him might think that he was looking at a daisy. But why would he want to do that? It is true that he could see a daisy, but the daisy had no meaning for him.

As it happened, two of his neighbours did see him there. In the twilight Marian Peacock was doing some late weeding after supper at the front, taking out the sturdy green plugs that flourished like parasites on her dry pale lawn, and Father Eustace across the road was looking out of his kitchen window, running the tap to fill his kettle. To him, Graham appeared to be miming something for children, as though in a game of charades, perhaps playing the role of Nebuchadnezzar. The words in Daniel rose to the priest's lips: "That very hour the word was fulfilled concerning Nebuchadnezzar; he was driven from men and ate grass like oxen; his body was wet with the dew of heaven till his hair had grown like eagles' feathers and his nails like birds' claws." The image in his mind was William Blake's, except that Graham Horrocks was bald and clothed. And there were no children about, so his neighbour couldn't be playing. And Graham didn't like the neighbourhood children anyway. Perhaps he was weeding, like Marian, except that she was wearing a little soft hat and big gloves, and stood staring at her lawn for much of the time, holding a special sort of weeding knife. Graham on the other hand was moving very slowly and uncertainly, with his head hanging down.

Before long Father Eustace returned to Yarnfield Close from Babylon and realised that Graham was unwell, since Marian had quickly run to her neighbour, was talking to him quietly and helping him to lie down.

Between them they called an ambulance, and within the hour Graham was in A & E at the John Radcliffe, with a suspected stroke.

2.

Arlene didn't think of herself as being really homeless. She was a free spirit, that's what she was. She had lived with Gizz on his houseboat for, oh, ever so long really, long enough to have discovered all about his unusual needs, and to find some of them what you might call unwelcome. He was overweight, and didn't seem to mind the houseboat being dirty. He also made a pretence of not minding when she said at the outset that she wanted to keep to herself. He was a greedy bastard, too, and there was always plenty of food on board. He liked those baked beans with little sausages in them, which she thought were in their own way perfectly acceptable in the circumstances, and sometimes on a fine evening, sitting on the roof among the tubs of flowers with a joint, they could joke and sing together. Not bad, you'd think. And he had this plan, which he might outline when he was clutching his third Heineken, of actually at last really and truly getting the engine fixed and puttering northwards up the canal to see how far they could get.

"What for?" Arlene would ask. "What might you be expecting to find?"

"No expectations, no disappointments," Gizz might reply, with a smile. And that seemed to be his philosophy of life.

Arlene decided that this way of thinking, though on the face of it compatible with her having long assumed the role of a free spirit, was in Gizz's case hypocritical, since his unusual needs showed themselves at largely inappropriate moments and revealed quite decidedly lewd expectations. Expectations of her and her kindly attentions in particular, implicitly in gratitude for beer and baked beans with little sausages in them, and for her being on the houseboat at all in the first place, which was not of his asking, was it?

Once her curiosity was satisfied and it seemed that Gizz's jokes were running out, Arlene decided to move on. The stove caught fire one morning, too, and though Gizz managed to put it out, the boat was left in a fine old state, and Arlene was left coughing her lungs up. That was it. The next time Gizz shambled into town to see what he could find, she was off. She was picked up by two mad students in an inflatable dinghy with an outboard motor thinking of making their way to Port Meadow for lunch at the Perch.

She had a laugh with them all right. She guessed that they too had their own unusual needs, but they were shy with each other in her presence, and nothing happened. They surely thought, though, that something might be going to happen at some point, because they gave her some money when she asked for it, which Gizz had never done because he never had any. She gave them each a merry little kiss.

What was she going to do? Her backstop was her friend Rose Daly, who had part-time work at a nearby pub and lived in Jericho. That was the reason for taking off with the students in the first place, otherwise she might have ended up almost anywhere, with nowhere to stay. There were favours here and there that she could call in, not all of them in convenient places, but she had some of her belongings stowed with one of them.

By the end of the day she had met up with Bambi, who was living in a tent in the old cemetery off Walton Street. Rose said he was a poet, and they all had a laugh about that because poetry was silly and boring, wasn't it, but Bambi had a lovely light in his eyes when he smiled. Rose got rather drunk, which didn't endear her to her boss, the proprietor. He obviously thought that a barmaid getting drunk on the job was like a bank clerk helping herself to tenners. What's more, he suspected her of giving free drinks to her friends. But since she was still fending off his hand

66

down the back of her jeans with relatively good humour, she could somehow get away with it.

St. Sepulchre's was as dank and gloomy as most cemeteries are, and it gave Arlene the heebie-jeebies. But she was glad she had now encountered Bambi. And his tent. It was, on the whole, a much better arrangement than Rose's floor. So, farewell to Rose, too, for the moment.

Being with Bambi felt like having something to nurture. If you were given a fragile pot plant you would know you had to water it and put it in the best bit of sunlight you could find. His whole body was like a stem, bent forward a little as if through growing too quickly. Shoulders rounded, to protect the vulnerability that was forced to face the world. The chest as flat as the stomach, one continuous tenderness almost without bone or muscle, his tracksuit bottoms loose on his hips.

He was entirely concave, where Gizz had been convex, and he projected a natural melancholy that was self-perpetuating and largely unavailable to good cheer, though he certainly wasn't above managing a few wry jokes. He accepted embraces without fervour, only a steady stare over her shoulder into what must have looked like an intolerable future. But he did accept them, and they made their way across Oxford together, camping in unlikely secret places that he either already knew about or had an unerring instinct for.

He coughed a lot, a deep dry silent cough that shook his whole body, and then seemed to leave him with the shivers. He didn't seem to be at all well.

"You're ill, aren't you," she accused him.

"Not in perfect health, no," he replied. "Why would I be?"

"What is it?"

"Everything you can think of," he replied. "Including a hole in the heart."

"Truly?" she said, in alarm.

'On a good day," he replied, "you can see right through it to the earthly paradise."

On their third night, walking up the Banbury Road, he suddenly threw the folded tent and all his other gear over a fence and climbed over it himself. When she followed him, she found that they were hidden at the back of a deep garden border beneath a pine tree in the formal grounds of St. Hugh's College.

"My own God, Bambi," she said. "We'll be found here soon enough, won't we?"

"It's out of sight, look, with the bushes," he replied. "We can't be seen."

"I hope you're speaking truth," said Arlene. "They'll maybe set the savage dogs on us."

"There are no dogs here," he said. "This is a place of learning, that's what it is. No dogs."

It was that night, during their postponed sleep beneath the deathless legend "Quechua", which she felt labelled them like some intrepid expedition in the Andes, that he told her of his life and troubles.

What could she say? It was an old story, one which even she had encountered versions of in her time: the tyranny of his mother's boyfriend, the boyfriend's abuse of his sister, the resort to drugs, the break-up of the family, the landlord selling up, his sister escaping, his mother in hospital, himself in hospital, the boyfriend beating him up. Bambi's voice persisted in the darkness like an interminable summary of some grinding TV soap which she had never seen and therefore couldn't really visualise. She stroked Bambi's arm as he talked, but she sometimes got lost in the pronouns, and before she had quite understood how his mother had died she had fallen asleep.

He remained a mystery to her. His name itself was a mystery. She asked him next day why he was called "Bambi."

"It's Disney," he said. "The little deer's mother was shot."

"But he didn't shoot your mother, did he?"

"He might just as well have done."

A school friend, a posh girl who was always looking out for him, had named him Bambi. She had given him a book about Pooh, who was also Disney. Arlene thought she knew all about Disney, but the bear in the book didn't look like Disney's bear at all. The pictures were really tiny and old-fashioned. She imagined the school friend as being tiny and old-fashioned as well, prim in a flowery frock, but Bambi said no, she was really really nice. And then Arlene felt a strange feeling that she had never felt before, of hatred for this schoolgirl, and a resentment of Bambi for sticking up for her.

Well, she hadn't stuck by Bambi, had she, the cow? She had stayed in her safe fancy house playing with her teddy bears, or pulling on her gumboots to go for walks in the rain, and having afternoon tea. Arlene had looked into the Pooh book for long enough to know that she hated all that, too.

But Arlene would stick by Bambi, right enough. Despite the Quechua tent, he didn't look as though he could take care of himself, so she could do it. She told him he should really watch that nasty cough of his, and get a check-up with a doctor. She would make him get a check-up. A hole in his heart? What was that, then? It was all right to turn it into a joke, but it sounded like the sort of thing that could cause you to drop down lifeless without warning, it did for sure.

She could get them both to the hostel and discover from Grazyna how Bambi could eventually find a job. Grazyna might even know (yes, she would know all right!) how Bambi might enrol somewhere to study whatever it was that was in that other book of his, the one with all the equations, which she hated almost as much as the Pooh book, but which she tolerated because it seemed serious and unknowable, and because it was somehow in Bambi's mind that that was what he might be doing. The thought of Gizz ever doing anything at all made her laugh. And after all, men should have their own occupations. Certainly, they should.

"You were good at school then, were you?" she asked him.

"You might say so," he said delicately. "But I got into trouble."

"Ah, trouble," said Arlene. "Don't we know all about that. Those places breed trouble right enough. It's their speciality."

"It wasn't my fault."

"To be sure it wasn't. Is it ever? They're institutions, aren't they? They need to have their victims."

Establishing Bambi as a victim in every area of his life gave Arlene the complete conviction that it was now her duty to take him in hand. She told him about the hostel, where there was always food and showers if you wanted, and help in finding work. She told him about OxSPOT, and Recovery, and almost convinced herself that this was a resource that she believed in and that she might at some point have to take up herself.

But when Bambi said "And what about you?" she fell silent. It was the same when he had asked her about her own past life, which at least out of politeness she could see that he was obliged to do, though he wasn't all that persistent in asking. And she always had her answer ready.

"You don't need to know anything about me. I am not known about. No history. Cheerful, me."

But Bambi wasn't cheerful. He was troubled. He had been living for a while in a doorway in Walton Street, trying to make enough money from passers-by to get to Reading, where he thought his sister was still living. This seemed reasonable to Arlene. But he didn't actually seem to have any money. She thought that whatever he might have scraped together had gone on drugs, because she soon found him shooting up. When he offered the needle to her she refused it, saying that she didn't want to go down that road, thank you. He didn't offer again.

It soon became clear that there was another idea in his head, which was to return to Cutteslowe to kill his mother's boyfriend, always presuming that he could be found. Perhaps he would do that and then go to Reading. He also had a friend Rick who lived in Marston, and Rick might give him some money. He thought they might cross Oxford through the Parks and walk up by the Cherwell and through the Marston fields.

Arlene laughed at this.

"What do you think you're going to kill him with?" she asked.

"I'll hypnotise him," said Bambi. "And he'll die of shame."

Arlene couldn't imagine Bambi hurting a fly, but the Marston friend sounded like a good prospect. Why didn't he want to try the hostel? When she asked him he simply batted the question back at her, and she had no answer either. But she would follow him and look after him. That much seemed decided. If anything serious should happen between them of a truly tender kind, that might be quite something. Despite being by nature a free spirit, she would keep a very open mind about that sort of fine prospect.

She was surprised at his resourcefulness. His knapsack was full of food stolen from the bin at the back of Londis: bruised fruit, out-of-date pasties and dead tuna sandwiches. Since he never seemed to eat, she wondered why he bothered. But of course, it was there for when he needed it, and she herself was always ready to eat at any time.

The river, when they found it, was a very different passage of water from the canal. On the canal you always felt that you were there on sufferance. Even taking to the water for the purpose of mere pleasure (like the mad students in their dinghy) became an intrusion into a world of purposeful and licensed river craft. Gizz was always in trouble about his mooring rights, and was harassed by the canal authorities. Along its course were disused factories and boatyards, tenuous reminders of its past history as a system of transport.

But the river was pure recreation, filled with the self-conscious shouts and splashes of undergraduates and the cautious pleased excursions of tourists. It had trampled margins where cows came to drink, and reedy enclaves where swans nested. There were fallen branches half across it, which no one had any need to clear away. It was a margin of the city that seemed to have nothing to do with the city, whereas the canal still felt like an old artery.

As they walked, Arlene tried to get him to talk about things, about all the failures of the system that prevented him from settling, from getting a job and a future. But Bambi didn't talk much during the day. He plodded on ahead up the riverside path, taking short-cuts through tall grasses and pausing occasionally to disentangle his rolled-up tent from an overhanging branch. Arlene followed, chewing hawthorn leaves, stopping to look at baby ducks. And if he did ever talk, he never seemed concerned about his future, only about the past. She would try to fire him up with stories of injustice and of all the impediments that lay in the way of getting any money or assistance, and all he could think about was what he had already lost. He was like a walking ghost from his own unhappy past.

He produced some dry sausage rolls. She ate one, and he showed her some things he had written in pencil on smoothed-out cardboard sandwich packaging. She thought they were the saddest words she had ever read, like little cries of help from a boat in the open sea. She hugged his elbow then, and in her unaccustomed surge of sympathy felt like a bride in a newspaper photograph. She was going to stick by him.

In a distant corner of one field they passed some people bellowing and playing with a frisbee. There were others seated around, pretending to listen to the stumbling chords of a guitar that had been brought for show and that no one could play. They were so far away, that when Arlene and Bambi saw their punt moored nearby, tucked into the bank by its pole and its rope loosely knotted to an alder, they climbed into it, squelched the pole out of the mud, unfastened the rope and pushed off.

Bambi had no idea how to punt, so it was Arlene who took them clankily zig-zagging upstream, laughing at their clumsiness and resourcefulness. They expected to hear shouts behind them, or angry figures appearing at the riverside, but they had not been seen.

"It's all right up here, isn't it?" said Arlene, when they had stopped again for a while. Bambi agreed. Being in the punt had relaxed him. Without the need to press on with physical effort, putting one foot in front of the other, he lost any sense of urgency. Where, indeed, had he decided to go?

Was it to Rick in Marston, where he might claim a few quid for old times' sake, or even a roof over his head, and perhaps some heroin? Or was it to Cutteslowe to trace his nemesis and destroy him? Arlene smiled at him as they rehearsed these possibilities. He hadn't decided yet whether to make a decision or not.

"Why decide?" said Arlene. "Just do whatever it is. That's what I do, for certain."

They lost all sense of where they were. They had left the last colleges and playing fields, and passed under a bridge where the pole hit the underside of the arch and their voices echoed thunderously at each other as cars hummed above them. It was only later, after a riverside pub where more punts were tethered, that Bambi began to wonder if they had gone too far.

"Who's to say so, and why would you believe them?" Arlene called out to him. He was stretched out in the punt and looked as though he might easily go to sleep. She laughed.

"Go to sleep, my weary hobo," she sang to him, with a deep thrust of the pole. She had got the hang of the punting now, and their steady onward progress was itself lulling.

But after some time, when the riverside path had disappeared and there was no one else on the river, with fields on either side of them, they agreed that they might have come too far.

"We should have stopped at the bridge," said Bambi. "It must have been the Marston road."

"Let's see," said Arlene. "Look, there are houses up there on the left."

"Let's go back," said Bambi. But they didn't go back.

They found a place on the left bank to tie up their punt as securely as they could.

"Too bad if someone takes it," said Arlene. "We took it ourselves, after all."

They crossed a field in the direction of the houses they could see, and eventually came to a path which bordered their back gardens. The walls and fences were high, as if to shield the houses from prying eyes. As if anyone ever walked along here, Arlene thought. It was dead quiet.

They explored the path, which didn't lead to anywhere very promising, and then walked back.

Arlene was tired after all that pole lifting, and thought that they might put up Quechua somewhere, and spend the night. Bambi protested at that, saying that they didn't know where they were. They argued for a while, with Arlene saying that it didn't really matter where they were, and Bambi pretending that he knew where he wanted to get to. He had decided after all that he would like to find his sister.

"Well, you're not going to get to Reading tonight, are you?" said Arlene. But she didn't want to quarrel with him. She felt like one of those persistent women in adventure films who are ignored by the hero all the way through, but stick by him against all odds; who just won't go away even when they are told to, and in the end are on the spot just in time to rescue him. She didn't want to help him to get to Reading because she knew that she could be a better sister to him than his real sister, who had thought to save her own skin and not looked out for her brother at all.

At the same time, she didn't feel exactly like a sister. All day whenever she had touched him her hand had wanted to stay there or move to another part of his body. She wanted it to pass over the white expanse of his belly. She thought it might be time to pitch camp again. In the end he agreed.

They found a patch of fence already partly collapsed, and it was easy to pull the wooden strips apart and get through. Bambi thought that they'd be safer in there than outside by the path, and once they'd squeezed in Arlene agreed that they would be well hidden. It was practically a jungle in there, more like another field than a garden. Perhaps it was a vacant building plot. They were even more concealed beneath the bushes than they had been at St Hugh's.

"We need some water," said Bambi. "There must be a way through to the houses."

That evening, before the sun set, and for a while afterwards, by the light of a torch, Bambi read aloud from *The House at Pooh Corner*. Arlene thought it was weird, these toy adventures and quaint conversations about almost nothing between a mind-wandering bear and an earnest piglet. She was sleepy lying by his side, with her right hand already where she knew it wanted to be.

It was altogether lovely, she thought, and they might settle here for a good long time. Better than Bambi going off to confront his past. He needed the future instead, and she could be his future.

The Piglet was being very timid, and the Bear was trying to be persistent. Was this Pooh story like them, she wondered? She didn't think she was like the Piglet, and despite the fact that they both made up songs she didn't think that Bambi was like Pooh either. He was much more like Eeyore.

Arlene became worried for Bambi. They were close in the tent, and that was quite fine by her she thought, for what might occur in the darkness there with the two of them like cheese and ham in a sandwich, and time stopped in the dead of night in that wild garden. But the closeness told her more than she needed to know about the state he was in, his breathing, his coughing, the blood in the morning across his sleeve.

"My own God, Bambi," she said. "You're hardly the picture of health. What are we to do with you?"

"You can tear me up in little pieces and throw me away."

"I'm not going to throw you away for heaven's sake. What's the good of that? And I thought you were aiming to kill your mother's boyfriend?"

"He'd be more likely to kill me. I'm half-way dying as it is."

"Don't talk like that. And you shouldn't always be sleeping in damp gardens for that matter. Could we not go back to Jericho? Rose Daly took a great shine to you, she did so. She'd give us her floor."

No answer.

"Are you asleep now, Bambi? Ah, so you're not asleep. What are we going to do? I thought you were a man with a mission."

"I'm probably more like a man with an emission."

"You're leaking all to pieces, Bambi. When the shops open I'll be off to buy you some linctus. Have you got any money left?"

No answer.

"Well, I'll buy you some linctus with my own money, such as it is. That's what I'll have to do. Then we'll get you to a doctor."

Arlene liked both the sound and the idea of the word *linctus*, a thick treacly word that would join things up that were in danger of falling apart. She thought of linctus as something to warm the cockles of the heart. Wasn't that something her mother used to say? Did she used to say it about soup, maybe? Soup was nourishing. But soup takes time on the stove. No stoves in these parts, no stoves any more, breaking down the bones, producing globules of fat. That'll stick to your ribs! That was what her father said, but it was so long ago.

That'll stick to your ribs, right enough. That'll warm the cockles of your heart. Who said such things any more? And why cockles?

Cockles and mussels. A cock was a muscle, wasn't it, rising like a helmeted warrior? As for a cockle, that was just like a scroodle berry, wasn't it? So that's what the song was all about: sweet Molly Malone singing cockles and mussels. The old story.

Arlene was drifting into sleep, considering the purchase of linctus, conveniently bottled and thick as soup, which would stick to Bambi's ribs and do him a world of good. She was aware how strange it was that for once she was proposing to spend her own money on a boy she had picked up instead of getting money from him. Did Bambi really have no money? Could there be somewhere he was hiding it? If he got any he'd only be using it to get a fix or to go to his sister in Reading. And Arlene wouldn't be wanted there.

It was no wonder he was so ill and thin, picking just at the insides of out-of-their-sell-by sandwiches. People are like what they eat, aren't they? Gizz with his beer and beans, bloated all the time, gas escaping from both ends like the sound of a motor boat. Typical English fart when you think about it. And then there are those tight little Japanese, all wrapped up like their black rice parcels, and Italians looking as though they've just been fried in olive oil. That fat priest she saw in the street liked his pudding all right, she could tell. Puddings made in the very shape of stomachs, round and full, and his face there, red as the holy wine. No ribs showing on that priest, bet you. But she could count the ribs on Bambi. They needed gluing together. Linctus, that was it. Heal the cough and stick to the ribs at the same time

As she became drowsier, her hand went out to find the ribs and counted them, like a little old woman made of her own fingers, walking up his chest. His breathing rattled, and though she thought perhaps they would need to get help soon, she was worried that he might easily become too ill to move on at all.

Later, although she thought he was asleep, he suddenly said:

"I couldn't ever actually kill anyone, you know."

3.

Father Eustace had reached the age when he couldn't sleep. For a time, he thought something might be wrong, checking over his bodily tics and aches as he stared at the ceiling. Eventually he decided that since he no longer enjoyed the slumbers of perfect health he might as well recognise what he knew to be a fact: that the natural biorhythms divided the night in two and made three o'clock a natural waking time. People had risen at that hour, busied themselves for a time, and then returned without anxiety for their second sleep. Why shouldn't he do the same?

He would turn on his bedside light and pick up his Dante, which he was reading with the assistance of the Carlyle-Okey-Wicksteed translation as a crib. He had read no modern translations, and indeed largely favoured Binyon and Sayers, but a prose translation was more honest, and he found the summaries and notes useful as a prod to his holiday Italian. He began Canto xxiii of the Paradiso in English:

> As the bird amidst the loved foliage who hath brooded on the nest of her sweet offspring through the night which hideth things from us,

who, to look upon their longed-for aspect and to find
the food wherewith to feed them, wherein her heavy toils
are pleasant to her,

foreruns the time, upon the open spray, and with
glowing love awaiteth the sun, fixedly gazing for the dawn
to rise;

so was my Lady…

What a marvellous epic simile for the watchful Beatrice, he
thought! But he himself, with no sweet offspring, was not going
to wait until dawn. He would get up and make himself a cup of
camomile tea and bring it back to bed.

In the kitchen Effie looked up eagerly from her basket, with a
little whimpering interrogation.

"Oh, do go back to sleep," said Father Eustace. "I'm not going
to start taking you for walks at this time of night."

Effie's tail thumped in eager contradiction.

"Am I?" smiled Father Eustace. "Oh dear. Am I going to have
to? Yes, I suppose I am. Why not indeed?"

As the kettle boiled, he thought not about Effie's desire for
night walks, nor indeed about Beatrice, but about the missing
homeless boy. He was uneasy. He was used to dealing with such
problems at the hostel, where Grazyna, being a good Catholic
herself, gave him a free run to bring comfort and a holy word to
those unfortunate enough to be compelled to seek shelter there.
It was all entirely unofficial for all sorts of reasons which he readily
admitted, such as that many of the "clients" (as they seemed to
have to be called these days) were Muslims.

Or that there was the possibility of a sly Anglican objection.
He thought that the ministers of the Church of England were on
the whole much happier attending to the souls of the middle-
classes than to those of society's outcasts (he was wrong) and
thought that if required he himself would readily wash the feet of
lepers or their equivalents (he was wrong about this, too). At any
rate, no Anglican objection was forthcoming.

So he turned up regularly at the hostel to give succour to Grazyna in return for slices of carrot cake, and occasionally had the opportunity to put his hands on the shoulders of young homeless men (as he had done with Michael Horrocks after his sermon on Matthew 24.43) and look with encouragement into their drug-distorted pupils.

But when one day he had found Grazyna closeted with an Irish girl who was claiming that her great friend had actually gone missing in Yarnfield Close, he was assailed by a strange feeling of worry and irritation unlike his usual benign and generalised concern. It was one thing to read about families being housed in shipping containers, and to deal with similar problems of homelessness at the hostel or even directly in the city's shop doorways, but to be confronted with a problem belonging to his own quiet neighbourhood was quite another. And he knew that Grazyna was taking it seriously because this time she had forgotten to give him any cake.

"The boy not here," said Grazyna, in her decisive tenor voice. "This young woman here, Eileen? Sorry, Arlene, she think he disappear up in Yarnfield Close, where you live yourself, right?"

"So it would appear," said Father Eustace. "But I don't see why."

"Look at this paper she bring," said Grazyna. "Arlene say the boy told her his tent stolen by this man described here with this address, Mr Graham K Horrocks, tent stolen with more poems written on these throw-away papers, am I right?"

She looked at Arlene for confirmation, and Arlene nodded. The girl seemed slightly traumatised.

Father Eustace looked at the sheet of paper: the familiar red-and-black logo of the building society that he himself used, with Graham's address in the upper left-hand corner and reference number 980546710 on the right, with below it the acknowledgement of his initial investment and the injunction to keep the document in a safe place. Why did the girl have Graham's details like this? Had the paper been stolen? Or was it just the tent that was stolen? Why should Graham have thrown the sheet away, he wondered? On the reverse was a poem, of sorts:

When two walk.   at first they walk
one in front   one
behind   who is the leader?
when two walk together
they are side by side
for ever

Father Eustace's memory was immediately stirred by all this.
He had not gone up to the end of the garden to see the tent and
Graham's papers discovered at the Close party, but of course he
had heard about it. He had got the impression that it was Bill
Peacock who was going to do something about it, and that Phyl
Jordan didn't want him to. If it was Bill who took charge of the
tent, presumably he would still have it. He said so.

"Not so much the tent," said Grazyna. "But where's the boy?"

Arlene spoke up.

"When we went back to the tent, his poems had gone. They'd
been taken. Except this one. He thought they'd been taken by this
man, right? He lives like just next door. He hated us. We went off
to get some chips. Next thing we find the tent gone too.
Everything. I thought we should go back to Rose's."

It took some time for Father Eustace to get it all straight. They
had a boat of some kind and were going downstream to find a
friend in Marston? Who was Rose? The girl had said forget about
the tent: if they've taken it, they've got rid of it by now. But the
boy went back to look for it, was that it?

"I was sick," said Arlene. "I was physically sick. We were back
at Rose's. I didn't go with him. Who would do that to us? We
weren't in anyone's way."

"Well, perhaps he didn't bother to look for it after all, then,"
Father Eustace had suggested.

"He would have come back to Rose's, surely," said Arlene. "I
should have gone back with him. I waited for him. I wasn't well.
I was sick. And he was very ill anyway."

"When was all this?"

"Last Tuesday," said Arlene.

Grazyna looked enquiringly at Father Eustace, who shrugged.

"I don't see what can be done about it now," he said. But in his mind he was turning over elements of the confusing story, not least the fact that Graham had gone into hospital on that very Tuesday. Father Eustace had travelled with him in the ambulance, and had later liaised with Marian about ringing Graham's children and seeing that the house was safely locked. How strange that this was apparently the day when the homeless boy had gone to see Graham about his tent, gone in fact to accuse him of having taken it.

"Please," said Arlene. "Father."

This quiet address stirred him at last in that well-hidden recess within his public persona that acknowledged a vocational duty. "Father"—indeed. She was, he thought, one of the city's lost children whom he was bound to take into his care. He couldn't deny her his help, but he had no idea what he might actually do. He promised her that he would make enquiries. Graham was coming out of hospital soon, and would presumably be able to say if he had seen the boy. And Bill: surely Bill wouldn't have thrown the tent away? Perhaps the boy had since come back again and reclaimed it? Perhaps he had even wanted to leave Arlene without having the courage to tell her? He still didn't know who Rose was.

As for Grazyna, she had too many other things on her mind. Not so much the usual troubles of her clients (the old men who turned up drenched in urine that was not their own; the policing of drugs; the pacifying of the police) but her own troubles. Why was she being harassed about her own status as an immigrant when everyone knew what a good job she was doing here? No one else would do it. This wasn't a city of people who did things. They were all thinkers rather than doers. Like the priest, who didn't like to get his hands dirty. She felt that in this case she had at least done her primary duty by getting Father Eustace involved, even if he would have forgotten all about it by tomorrow. That ended the matter.

For the time being, however, Father Eustace was rather more involved with Dante. It would be, he felt, something of a dramatic surprise if he were to deliver a sermon on a text not from the Bible but from Dante's *Divine Comedy*. He would take as his theme the vision shown to Dante by Beatrice when ascending to the constellation of Gemini, that of the tiny earth below him as "l'aiuola che ci fa tanto feroci." This line from the Paradiso 22.151 was something of a crux, out of which he thought he might contrive a significant argument. Was it "the flower garden that makes us so fierce" or "the threshing-floor that makes us so fierce"? Dictionaries seemed to provide either interpretation of the word, and one might think that it didn't matter, since the point was that in such a cosmic scale the earth is pathetically tiny, making warfare ridiculous, like bald men fighting over a comb.

Really, Father Eustace decided, the point of the word was the diminutive. It was simply a "little area", from the Latin *areola*. The earth was truly small, after all. But for a sermon he knew he could make great play with the alternative translations. In effect, the earth could be both a garden and a threshing-floor (a translation introduced by Longfellow), both of them places of the moral testing of the Christian soul, the temptation in Eden and the symbolic winnowing of the Last Judgement, first things and last.

Father Eustace took great pleasure in imagining the effect of all this on his congregation. For finally, surely, he thought, among all the vain national struggles and ceaseless petty global conflicts that surround us, which we seem powerless to avert, there is at the heart of it one inescapable truth: the individual soul must be judged.

He saw himself in the carved pulpit, raising first one hand then the other, like a conjuror pronouncing the absence of deception, an orator secure in his inescapable dialectic.

The business of a missing boy in his street could wait.

E ach day when Graham woke seemed like a new life. At first, in the hospital, the light touching and defining the corner of a cupboard, a door, or a monitor, brought with it no description of the thing. The shape had no identity or focus, so that he could stare at a curve and not know if it were a towel on a chair or his own hand just a few inches from his cheek. That strange pale outline of a rigid head and shoulders, frighteningly still, turned out to be just the space between the blinds and an oxygen cylinder.

There were no words attaching themselves to these appearances, even when after a few minutes they resolved themselves into perspective and familiarity. He was content to learn again, slowly, the lineaments of the world in which he found himself.

There was Susan, telling him things that were of no interest whatsoever, apparently leaving his bedside only quite suddenly turning out to have been there all along when he opened his eyes again. Or to be just as suddenly not there when he opened his mouth to say the words that wouldn't come. Did he know she was Susan? Sometimes he thought she might have been only a nurse. She might even have been Maddie, except that after a while he remembered that Maddie was dead. Did she know she was Susan? Or was she a ghost?

But memories in general, seeing that they had no business with his body, continued to elude him. This new life was not only a strange life in a new place, it was a life of the body. His body had told him that he was mortal, and he had denied it. In denying his mortality he denied everything up to the point at which denial had become necessary, and for a time that included the names of things. He had come to think that since things were transient and unreliable they had no need of names. At one time everything had been a projection in his mind of things that he could indeed name, but that light had been switched off.

To wake each day without a name or history would be like becoming a baby, and he was treated like a baby. His body had no sense of self, and no sense of the future or the past. He was content to be rolled over and feel the nurse's damp flannel between his legs. He sipped liquid when the straw was put into his mouth. He was again helpless and innocent.

The voice of Susan was replaced by the voice of Michael, which seemed very strange to him, until he saw that it was accompanied by Michael's face, and that Michael was in fact sitting there by his bedside. Had he been there before? A face was much more credible than a voice, which so easily merged with the ambient sounds, and was lost. Yes, it was Michael.

Graham's lips formed words.

"I didn't…"

"What, dad?"

"I didn't hurt you, did I, Michael?"

"No, Dad."

What memory was that, struggling to be born? The face was Michael's, pale and thin, but with the thick Horrocks nose, and the deliberately unshaven chin. Did it remind him of a younger Michael? What did it remind him of?

"You're much better now, Dad," said Michael's face. "Look, you're talking."

Yes, he could talk. And walk. The doctors came round, and they too said he was much better. Although the hours could seem as long as days, and he had no tally of the days themselves, he suddenly felt in control again, and the future became a territory into which he might dare to step.

His TIA had been a significant one, he was told, but he was treatable with medication (aspirin and clopidogrel, the youngest of the doctors explained to him) and he was to go home. This, he began to see, was something which was not only now allowed, or indeed recommended, but something which he was going to have to do. And somehow he accepted the authority of this young doctor in a way he might not have done with Dr. Driffield, since it implied that his condition was indeed not serious, and could be left in the hands of a competent junior.

Susan reappeared, with much talk of having to get back to the boys, but it was Michael who stayed at his bedside, saying: "What are we going to do with you, Dad?" And it was Michael who organised the taxi to take them to Yarnfield Close, after Graham had inserted one trembling limb after another in to some clean clothes that he recognised with slight irritation as ones that he rarely, if ever, wore nowadays. There was a mirror in the ward, and Graham saw a vision of a man in strange greenish trousers and a fair-isle sleeveless jumper looking like an unconvincing waxwork of himself.

Back at the house, he sat sullenly in the living-room trying not to listen to his children making unconvincing plans for his convalescence. One of them would stay with him. A meal was prepared. He found Maddie's diary on the kitchen table and managed to hide it before Susan or Michael could see what it was. This, and evidence of other elements of his recent life, stirred him to confront his actions before going into hospital, which till now he had been suppressing. A necessary appointment had been made with Dr Driffield. But none of the three now talked very much, or knew quite what else to do.

Graham's not knowing what to do was of a different order from Susan's or Michael's. For now he had remembered precisely what had happened in the hour leading up to his little stroke on Tuesday, and the memory sat in his mind like an unwieldy structure that had somehow been placed there in error, and was preventing his life from joining up in the ordinary way. It was a structure that would be impossible to dismantle, but he could neither get past it to the ordinary life that he led before, nor move beyond it into a continuation of that life in the future. It was like a precarious scaffolding holding up a ruin. He could do nothing about it without the likelihood of total collapse, and yet nothing else could credibly be done while it was still there.

He saw the memory now for what it really was: the unfolding of events for which he was responsible, a disaster in his life which might easily have been averted; not only a nightmare which in his lost innocence he daily woke to, but an absolute and shocking event in the only world to which he belonged. It was an utter horror.

And now at home each morning was the same. From the wanderings and anxieties of dreams he would wake to the blank slate of his primal self. But this state was momentary. Before he had looked at his bedside clock, before he had even turned and stretched in bed, the realisation was upon him again. Some days ago now (how many days? Was it a week?) he had attacked the dosser when he found that he had broken into the pod. He thought he had inflicted a lot of damage, really a great deal of damage, since he was a strong heavy man and the dosser was nothing at all, a wasted body, frail and ill-nourished. He had certainly at least broken the boy's arm.

Since he didn't really want to think, he found little time to think. That was easy enough. He was always being brought cups of tea. Michael was still at Yarnfield Close, doing everything he could as often as he could (Graham thought) to make up for the fact that very soon he would feel that it was all right to be off and away. He even let in neighbours who had come round to see how his father was doing, when he could easily have kept them out. It was as though he had to demonstrate his willingness to be a carer, so that it could be remembered after he had gone back to London. They would readily say: "Wasn't Michael good to have stayed with him?"

And all this time Graham could not, or would not, go to the pod. The keys were still in his pocket, part of the belongings dutifully returned to him when he was discharged from the JR. No one else could have gone there while he was in hospital, and no one showed any interest in going now. Why would they? Michael shopped for him, and made coffee for Phyl Jordan and Marian Peacock when they came round with Marian's flapjacks, and spent most of his time on his iPhone placating what sounded to Graham like a very unhappy Koon-Mi at the other end.

What was he to do? Should he tell Michael everything and take him to unlock the pod and deal with what they might find there together? God forbid. He wanted Michael to go away. He was quite all right now, wasn't he? This was something he had to deal with on his own. And if he could be left to deal with it on his own, it might not be too bad. He could take the boy to hospital, give him money, see him right and make him keep quiet.

But wait. So many days had passed. How many days without water or food? And how badly injured? He wouldn't know until he went to open the pod.

And until he was to go to the pod, the nature of the problem and the degree of his guilt, by being unknown, would not yet seem quite real to him. There was a distinct part of his mind which clung, with apparent reason, to this helpful proviso. What would he find? He didn't know.

Any distraction helped. If Michael suggested watching a television programme, even if it was one he disliked, he would agree, because it filled the time with its nonsense, and he needn't pay any attention to the other part of his mind which was always there ready to niggle at him, saying: "Go there now, at all costs, before it is too late!"

With each bite of flapjack, his tongue feeling for the soft crumbs lodged between tooth and gum, he would smile and agree with Phyl's complaints about the national political impasse when in his heart he didn't agree at all because he knew that she wished to destroy the Conservative Party. To agree was no different from biting a flapjack. It was the comfort of normality. He agreed, too, with Marian when she said how relieved she was that Bill was not after all buying shares in Bullettpods. He even agreed with her when she complained that Bill ought to do more gardening, or at least water it in all this heat. It was not his real opinion, but he didn't want, out of a kind of superstition, to disturb the tranquil surface of the ordinary. He agreed with the flapjack, too.

When Father Eustace called, he brought no flapjacks, but he did bring with him a question that disturbed the tranquil surface.

"I've been asked if you know anything about the young man who was camping here at the end of last month," he said.

"Why should I know anything?" asked Graham, his heart beginning to sound in his ears. "What sort of thing?"

Father Eustace beamed with a reassuring and complicit bonhomie.

"I think we were all aware of them," he began.

Them? Though Graham, suddenly remembering the time that he had seen the pair walking down the Close.

"Yes," continued Father Eustace. "This young woman who was with him appears to believe that you took his tent."

"I haven't laid a finger on his tent," said Graham truthfully.

"Quite so," said Father Eustace. "I'm sure not. But she thought you had taken his poems as well. They were written on the back of some old papers of yours, which I suppose he might have taken from the recycling."

"That's rubbish," said Graham, immediately realising that several people at the Close party had seen him take them, though they wouldn't have known what they were.

"She said you had words."

"I did give him a pen," said Graham, as a concession to the truth.

"Ah," said Father Eustace. "To write the poems?"

"No," said Graham sharply. "Not to write the poems. He didn't say what he wanted it for."

"Oh," said Father Eustace, giving the impression that he thought Graham was perhaps being self-contradictory. "Well, it doesn't really matter, except that the boy has disappeared."

"Disappeared?" Graham felt irritated and on the defensive now. "Where from? Where the hell is he expected to be?"

Father Eustace raised his eyebrows at the tone of this response, but spread his hands placatingly on his knees as if quite satisfied and ready to depart.

"I suppose she feels that he was here at Yarnfield Close, and now isn't."

"Hardly surprising. He could be anywhere. And he had no need to be here, did he? No right to be here?"

"Indeed," said Father Eustace. "I'll have a word with Bill about that tent. I suppose they are those druggies you heard that time. They may have quarrelled, and he's taken off."

"I should think that's very likely," said Graham, in relief. "Very likely indeed. Not welcome here."

"Not welcome? I suppose not."

Father Eustace stood up. He knew that he wasn't getting anywhere.

"Talking of welcome," he said. "I must get back to Effie. She'll be very cross with me, and I must take her for a walk."

And off he went.

Once Michael, too, had left, with a promise to return at the next week-end, Graham was without distractions. But that didn't mean that he found himself able to act. On the contrary, he sank into a state of suspended animation, shuffling into the kitchen to make a cup of tea, going to bed early to stare half the night at the corner of his pillow. He almost wished that he had been kept in hospital, where he wouldn't have been required to do a thing.

One morning the phone rang and it was Con Bullett.

"I suppose you saw the *Financial Times* today?" said Con.

"It's not a paper I read, no," said Graham.

"You and Bill missed your chance there, old friend. The shares have gone to 42 right away. The Germans are extremely interested."

"Well, good luck to you, Con."

Graham wasn't going to admit that he hadn't bought any shares just because he couldn't raise the money in time.

"It's not luck, Graham," said Con smugly. "It's bloody hard work."

Graham was happy to think that Con would imagine that he, like Bill, had made a rational decision about the shares, and had erred on the side of prudence. That was better than being shown up as financially incompetent. But he was nonetheless enraged. And for a time, this rage seemed almost to justify his earlier anger and its consequences.

But soon enough he realised that the lost shares were no excuse for anything. In his present state he had gone far beyond excuses.

When he was twelve, his parents had given him a set of oil paints, to encourage him to be creative. He took them to school, to show them off, and not being creative barely used them there, as there was no real opportunity. He pretended to his parents, whenever they asked, that they were indeed useful and that he painted all the time in his free periods. Then one day he couldn't find them, and didn't know whether someone had taken them from his locker or they had just disappeared from the art room. In truth, he didn't care much, but whenever his mother mentioned them, he couldn't admit that he had lost them, and pretended that great paintings were in progress which he would ultimately bring home and show her. He maintained the pretence for months and months.

If guilt could be admitted, he now thought, it was half-way to being expiated. The visit of Father Eustace reminded him of the value which his church placed upon confession. But though Maddie had been a Catholic (of the cheerful misbehaving kind who liked to gossip about her sins in the course of putting them behind her) Graham belonged to no precise faith. He went to church because Maddie had done so, and because Father Eustace was such a very local feature. Susan and Michael had been baptised at his church, and Susan married there, so it was always pleasing to return with them and proudly put them on parade. He would never go to confession in a month of Sundays. Also, Maddie's crazy friend Caroline Boxwood was often there, a church groupie, and it gave him a conflicted thrill to see her, to imagine her body and to remember that Maddie had come to prefer to be with him.

He had not confessed the oil paints until it was no longer possible to claim that he still had them. As far as his parents knew, they were not missing. He hadn't reported them missing. Only the thief (presuming that there was a thief) knew it, and the thief wasn't going to say anything. So that in effect they were not missing. It was the same with the dosser in a way, though in something like the opposite way. He was thought to be missing, since no one knew where he was. But only Graham knew where he was. He was like that book in the Cambridge library that had been put back on the wrong shelf. And not only that, he could be rescued and restored, supposing it was not too late.

Why did Graham not go to the pod to see? He knew the reason in his heart. It was the same reason that had prevented him from confessing to his parents that he had lost the paints and then lied about them. He was frightened. If he had done something straight away, he thought, it was always possible that he would be immediately forgiven. Not exonerated perhaps, because then the sin is expunged from the record. But forgiveness is an act of grace.

Besides, if he had acted immediately in this case, things might not have gone so badly for the dosser. Graham could have said something to Michael while he was still at the hospital, and there would have been a third-party rescue, at least relieving him of the task of actually doing anything himself. He could have claimed the rights of a householder to defend himself against an intruder. He needn't confess anything at all.

But his state of panicked indecision had changed all that. However he might have explained his attack on the boy in the first place, deliberate though it was, an act of rage not calculated, not willed, but misguided and spontaneous, now this crucial and

90

protracted delay could not be said to be accidental. And after Father Eustace's visit, he knew it would be worse for him.

And he knew that his instinctive choice of delay was finally not only cowardice, but a kind of self-protection, a blocking of any route towards confession or forgiveness. The great structure in his mind that stood so heavily upon him and was preventing his life from proceeding in its usual channels was no lighter, but like some recognisable feature in his personal landscape it now bore a name. It was like an expected sign-post that he could now read with relief, and the sign read: "Not Yet."

It was a sign that anyone might live by. You needn't do anything yet. The worst is not over yet. Things are tolerable so far. Don't do a thing. Not yet.

It was also a step towards a further possible line of action, where fear turns into ruthless self-protection. For Not Yet can so very easily become Not At All.

The days were noticeably hot now. Lottie from Number 2 came back from Greece and said that the temperature hadn't been any higher over there. Colin Sherwood set up a sprinkler on the shared lawns which he moved about without turning off the water, stumbling about laughing and getting drenched. "Saves me going to the pool," he shouted. And Ann Sims was seen wearing an enormous straw hat with a silk scarf threaded through it, which Marian said must have belonged to her great-grandmother.

It had been no problem for Graham to put off going back to work. The department could cover for him, even if in the process they might discover how little he actually did and therefore how dispensable he was. He didn't want to leave the house, of course. He couldn't leave until his problem was resolved. He even let Marian do some shopping for him. Bill brought it round.

Marian had Bill twisted round her little finger as usual, he thought.

"That's really very good of you," said Graham.

"No problem," said Bill. "Sorry I haven't seen you properly since... you know, your thing."

"I haven't been very sociable, really."

Bill had seated himself in the kitchen, the bags of shopping still unopened on the table. He had known Graham for long enough to have "really and truly" forgiven him for once having tried it on with Marian. But as with that formulaic promise of childhood, it had been made somewhat under duress, or at least with an eye to some moral advantage. Things would not have been well with Marian if he had not seen fit to forgive Graham, since to forgive Graham was somehow to forgive Marian as well, which was certainly necessary for all concerned. Bill never wanted to be thought as easy-going as he appeared to be, but at the same time he preferred a quiet life, one that he could feel himself entirely in charge of.

What had been the circumstances? Indeed, it might have been nothing much. Maddie had been out with Susan at the clinic. Bill had gone to B & Q. It was a Saturday morning and Graham had called next door to see if Bill could lend him a sander. Marian had been late getting up and answered the door in a towelling bathrobe and mermaid hair. Were there any excuses for what may or may not have happened? They were all much younger then, when blind urges could take an indiscriminate grip on otherwise civilized persons.

Marian had always said that she found Graham creepy, and that earlier confession had somehow validated and excused her later one. Whatever didn't happen (or perhaps did happen) was somehow her fault, she engagingly claimed. After all, she needn't have answered the door. Bill had wondered if her saying so was designed to stop him from going round and knocking Graham's head off. If so, it was successful.

And so they had settled into middle-aged familiarity. It was perhaps like that with many neighbours. But Bill was pleased to think that Graham had missed out with Bullettpods when he had clearly wanted to buy them. He could waste his money in other ways.

Now, with Graham clearly breaking up physically, Bill could afford to patronise him. He looked round brightly.

"Quite an episode, wasn't it?"

"It was."

"Bit scary, I expect."

"Well, I'm still here."

In truth, Bill thought that Graham, despite his bluster, was simply weak. And now after his episode, he was showing it. Graham was irritable when he found that he couldn't manage his own affairs, like that business about losing his papers. He did little for himself. He'd try to borrow a sander instead of thinking of hiring one. He'd take another man's wife instead of looking after his own. Poor Maddie: it was probably Graham's shouting at her for all those years that gave her the tumour. Only weak men shouted. He even shouted at children. Marian said she thought that when Susan and Michael were grown up Maddie was going to leave him. Well, she did, didn't she, in a way? But not in the way she would have wanted.

"I wonder what triggers these things," Bill went on. "That evening it happened, you know. I was taking a leak upstairs and thought I heard something at the bottom of your garden, a bit of shouting. Was there a problem?"

Graham felt the blood drain from his cheeks.

"Really?" he said.

"Thought it might have been you," said Bill. "But I couldn't think what it was."

"Oh," said Graham noncommittally, trying to indicate a similar puzzlement.

Bill waited a second for an explanation, but then said:

"It was probably someone in the lane. We get all sorts there."

"We do, we do," Graham rapidly agreed.

"Anyway," said Bill. "Next thing I know, Marian's sending you off to A & E with old Eustace. And I thought she was just dead-heading the roses and weeding the front. Lucky she saw you."

"Oh yes," said Graham, gratefully steering the narrative back to the safety of his collapse and rescue. "Very grateful for that. And for once I can't say a word against the NHS."

"We're none of us getting any younger," said Bill, with a theatrical sigh. Then suddenly: "Oh, by the way, that tent, you remember? I took charge of it."

"Took charge of it?"

"Yes. Rolled everything up. The torch was quite a good one. Put it in the garage. Thought it might be evidence."

"Evidence?" said Graham, again alarmed.

Bill laughed.

"Well, I did ring the police," he said. "So instead of taking it to the dump I thought I'd better keep it. Not that the police will lift a finger. When I told them it was Yarnfield Close the sergeant said "Not again, sir" which I thought was really rude and useless. After all, it's plainly trespass. And those drugs you found."

"A syringe," said Graham.

"Yup," said Bill. "They need to do something about it. I might speak to someone higher up, in fact."

However he might have felt in the past about such a firm line of neighbourly action, Graham was now troubled by even this very unlikely prospect of police presence in the Close. But what would they think they could do? What would they actually be investigating? He was more disturbed by the thought that Bill had heard him shouting at the dosser. Of course he would have heard, with the pod door open. What might he have heard precisely from his upstairs bathroom window? Not very much, perhaps. It was too far away. And there was nothing more that Bill himself was now likely to do.

But what about Father Eustace? What was he now going to do? The tent was all wrapped up in more senses than one, and Bill would probably forget about it, but Father Eustace was pursuing a disappearance, and however vague and dilatory he was, that was in itself a more serious matter, and for a while at least Father Eustace might not forget it. Besides, hadn't he said that he would "have a word with Bill about that tent"? Two and two might be put together.

Graham thought it was unlikely that Father Eustace would ever get around to doing any such thing, and if he didn't, then nothing more would happen.

And what would happen anyway? In the early morning, with the July sunlight already bright between the gap in the bedroom curtains, he would wake, innocent for that blissful moment before the deadly realisation of his predicament descended upon him, and imagine that it was all still a dream. Of course, he even argued to himself, the boy could have managed to climb out of the Velux, not too badly hurt, and feeling guilty at his own trespass have gone far away without thinking to report Graham for assault or to make any sort of complaint. He had been so passive, hadn't he? Unlikely to retaliate. A fatalist. A loser.

But once Graham was out of bed and shaving, staring at his great red face in the bathroom mirror, he knew that he was deceiving himself. How could the boy have got up to the skylight? It was impossible. And if he had, he wouldn't then be thought to have disappeared, would he?

As he dressed, he tried to believe in his own safety. The furniture of his bedroom, so often a simple comfort after the victimisation and paralysis of nightmare, offered its familiar shapes and surfaces as if to console him. "Look, I am your chair," the chair would say. "I keep your clothes for you, your linen trousers over my seat, your pink shirt over my back. All is well. All is as it always is. You can take the clothes now and assemble yourself into your impregnable public self once more." But the consolation was false, just as false as nightmare was so often startlingly true, and Graham knew that his life had irrevocably changed.

And then one day Arlene came back to Yarnfield Close, making a bee-line for number 4.

Graham saw her out of the kitchen window coming up the path without any of the uncertainty of someone who is not sure what they might be coming for or who might feel that they shouldn't be there at all, but with the determined pace of a postman, who has a precise task at hand.

He recognised her from the time he had seen her with the dosser coming into the Close. She was tiny and hunched, and walked with her hands thrust in the pockets of her jeans. Her long dirty pale hair clung to her head and cheeks as though no breeze could ever lightly lift it. She had a sharp nose, and a rather distinctive small mouth, her lips compressed in intentness. Her walk was rapid and mechanical, shoulders hunched and still as she came towards the house.

Graham froze in alarm, and his piece of toast popped out of the toaster at the precise moment that the doorbell rang. The familiar noises were simultaneous, and if it hadn't been that girl at the door, but Phyl say, he might have laughed and said something to her about it when he opened the door.

As it was, he wondered why he opened the door to her at all, even as he did so. He could have stayed in the kitchen and done nothing, and she would have had to go away. Something in those concerted sounds had perhaps compelled action, like the opening chords in a piece of music.

When people say "Can I come in?" it is almost impossible to say no. She pushed past Graham and stood in his hallway.

"Nice pictures," she said, looking at the one on the back wall of two vermillion and lime-green dancers swooning over each other in a cellar. Graham had always hated it. It was one that Maddie had bought on a whim from what he thought was a pretty fly-by-night and overpriced gallery on the High Street.

"Nice houses, too," said the girl.

Graham could read the subtext here. Nice houses, and I'd like to come back in the night and burn them down.

"My name is Arlene Fallon, by the way," she said, and she sat down surprisingly on the chair in the hall even though it had a hessian shopping bag on it, and sat there as though in a waiting room ready for her name to be called or something else decisive to happen.

Graham was conflicted with anger and fear and a strange kind of attraction to this intruder. He certainly wasn't going to introduce himself in his own house to someone who had no right to be there. But he knew that she was the girl who had been to Father Eustace (how? where?) to report that her friend had disappeared. And if she was here, perhaps she had more of his missing papers with all his private details and her friend's "poems" scribbled all over them.

"I don't need to know your name, do I?" he said. "What do you want?"

The girl looked up at him searchingly, as if to discover in his face the guilty knowledge that would be the answer to her question before she needed to ask it. Then she looked away at the floor, as though formulating the question at all was useless.

"He came to you for things, didn't he, my friend Bambi?" she said. "He said he thought you hated him. He's very sensitive about things like that. The others were friendly."

The question was only a statement, though Arlene knew it was true enough. She didn't think it would lead to anything very helpful.

And Graham had really nothing to say. "The others?" Had this girl been visiting all his neighbours? Had she been getting them to say things about him? And what had she been telling them? Well, she knew nothing. It was hearsay. There was nothing to know. And "Bambi." What was that? It couldn't be the dosser's name. It was ridiculous. It was all pointless and ridiculous.

Seen close to, she was older than he had first thought. It was her slightness and her clothes that made her seem girlish, the cartoon t-shirt and frayed trainers, the contained walk, the underdeveloped figure. But her tired face had little lines at the eyes and mouth that suggested she might be over thirty. There was a cold sore on her lower lip.

Why was it, that despite these signs of poverty and deprivation, so pitiable if he had been able to yield himself to such a sentiment, he could not take his eyes from her? There was something about the way she sat there, directly challenging him in his own house, that put him in a state of helpless attention.

This paradox of vulnerability and sensuous presence reminded him of the old puzzle of the wildly varying characteristics of the women he knew and felt drawn to. Size was at the core of the conundrum. Maddie had been just the right size, and not just because he knew her best, and intimately, her head on his shoulder, his arms under and around hers. Mary Flint was quite small, but with the enormous breasts which had so disturbed him on that holiday in Cornwall. Phyl Jordan was taller than Maddie, and could be a bully. Caro Boxwood was a decidedly large woman, with intimidating talk and a jaw to match. In his fantasies he thought of himself as likely to give as good as he got.

But with this tiny Irish woman it was different. He didn't know her at all, but here she was, daring to appear in his house, clearly wretched in her way, but valiant, with her lucid Irish voice and shrewd foxy face. She had no one to look out for her, no one to appeal to. No one would miss her, just as no one else would miss her partner in vagrancy, this absurd "Bambi." He wanted to grip back her dirty hair and take her little face in his hand. He wanted to push her to the floor and choke the life out of her. And more.

But all this was only the slightest of intuitions of possibility creeping under his skin, fuelled by an irrational desire. He knew very well where his best interests lay now. With perfect politeness and icy propriety, he would field her impossible suggestions and questions, and send her packing.

And when he had managed to do so, he would at last do what he had put off for so long and so dangerously. He would that very day go down to the bottom of his garden and unlock the door to the pod. And so he did.

H e waited until it was dark, nearly eleven o'clock, before he went to the pod.

He had kept the keys in his pocket all this time so that there could have been no possibility of anyone else going there. He checked the sightlines from his neighbours' houses, particularly from the Sherwoods' on his left and the Peacocks' on his right, making sure that no one in an upstairs window could have a clear view of the pod. If a light were on it would be difficult to see out clearly, and if curtains were drawn nobody would be looking out in any case. He had been worried about Bill saying that he had heard him shouting, and knew that sound carried in unpredictable ways. But that was why Maddie had the pod soundproofed in the first place, and the soundproofing had worked.

The windows were all dark.

Here he was, just outside the pod in the warm night air, a torch ready in his pocket. He brushed away a fly from his forehead. The vegetation around him was quite still, in sculptured masses, and there was a scent on the air, perhaps from the lime tree in Ann Sims's garden.

98

His proposed action was simple, and yet not so simple. He was still gripped, as in life it must always be, by the nature of choice, which tells you that at every moment of decision the decision can be ignored. Even at this eleventh hour Graham could tell himself that what is not known may not have happened. His actions had had consequences, but by concealing them (or not revealing them) even he could not yet know what they were. And the action that is not yet performed may never have to be performed. He might, he thought, have another, possibly fatal, stroke at that very instant, and then he would never have to face the outcome of what he had done. He would never, that is, be able to put his decision into practice. His choice would remain unacted.

But even on unlocking the pod door, the challenging alternatives remained. Here he remembered again his incomplete understanding of Michael's illustration of quantum mechanics and the indeterminacy of the position of electrons, perhaps because Michael himself had not quite understood it, or had explained it badly.

The cat in the box was, in effect, neither alive nor dead: you could not know until the box was opened. The cat in the box! Graham had been so proud of Michael's progress at school. It hadn't seemed a day since he was more interested in the Cat in the Hat, but Dr. Seuss had been inevitably supplanted by Dr. Schrödinger. Why was Michael now such an aimless failure?

Reason told him that the dosser might have managed to drag the little chest of drawers underneath the skylight and to have climbed out; or that despite, what? nine or ten days without food or water, he would be still there and alive; or that he would be dead. These were the alternatives. But reason also told him something of the likelihood of each possibility, and his long delay had nothing to better that relative likelihood. His mind was a twisted rope of fear and hope.

He had trodden softly on the path in his rubber-soled shoes, and all was quiet except for the momentary distant wail of an owlet. There was a buzzing in his ears as he turned the brass mortice key in the lock. It made its inevitable click, which at that hour sounded so loud that he couldn't believe that it wouldn't bring his neighbours to their windows in curiosity. He paused before slowly opening the door.

The buzzing was suddenly louder, very much louder, and in the moment when he realised that it was coming from inside the pod and not from inside his head, he smelled the unmistakeable smell that pointed to the third alternative: death. Had he expected this? He had indeed feared it, and feared its growing likelihood the longer he had postponed his visit, with its vain and dwindling hope of some sort of rescue. But had he thought it certain? Or even likely? Even now, in this moment of shock, he didn't know.

It isn't often that the smell of death announces its message of bodily collapse on the passing air. The sheep broken in a fall in a valley, hidden in bracken. The mouse behind the kitchen unit, trapped when Graham had filled in the old vent outside.

Decomposition sends out a passing signal that all living creatures recognise and that most will shun. It is a sweet smell, sweet as though in the hideous metamorphosis of death the warmth and motions of the ended life are distilled and commemorated. But it also has the acrid smell of the elemental in to which all living matter breaks down, and because it is ready to break down there will be some creatures attracted to it.

The flies were thick in the pod, circulating wildly in the air and hitting his head. They rose from the floor, darting across the beam of his torch. Their accumulated hum became even louder as he moved cautiously inside, as though beyond their angry darting they celebrated a purposeful activity like the sound of the communal mower on the Yarnfield front lawns.

The body was much where he had left it, by the rear wall, on its back, with arms splayed upwards like branches, hands cupped to the air with white distinct fingers. The posture itself was frightening and incongruous, like a gesture in ballet. The phrase "rigor mortis" entered Graham's confused head, but when he dared to bend and push at the fingers with his torch the arm fell slowly back.

He moved the beam of his torch across the swarming body to the boy's face, as though to confirm, as if he needed to, that this dead thing was who he expected it to be, the very person he had left here, damaged, and not someone for whom he might suddenly and gratefully feel no responsibility at all.

The face was moving.

Moving, yes, but it could hardly now be said to be anything like a face. The maggots pulsed and rode over each other, glistening in the eye sockets, seething where there had been cheeks, filling the gaping of the mouth. They were about the length of his thumbnail, most of them, though some, over-riding the others, were larger. Some dripped to the floor.

For a moment Graham's general thoughts and intentions were entirely lost to him in the wonder he felt at this blind and merciless activity. Nothing in human life that he was familiar with had any parallel to this writhing theatre, hidden until his torch had shone on it, and now quite unresponsive to his transfixed gaze. This was action without delay, intention without distraction, self-preservation without guilt. This was nature at her cruellest. Beside it, even Graham's murderous release of rage had been purposeless and trivial. He did not need to know any of the facts behind this performance, that 300 eggs can hatch within a day, that maggots simultaneously breathe and eat, that they can consume up to 60 per cent of a body in less than seven days, and after nine turn into flies. All he knew was that in one blind minute he had set this process in motion, and now he was left with it.

Back in the house, still trembling at what he had seen and what he must now deal with, Graham sat in the kitchen with a scotch. He could see that there were still a few lights on in the Close, the Terrys' across the way, for instance. They were probably waiting for Sharon to get back from some rave. She was far too young to be up so late. He knew that Ann Sims left her hall light on all night, to deter burglars. But he must wait till much later before doing anything. There was a still point in the middle of the night when no one could possibly be about and no one wakeful enough to be bothered to investigate even the slightest noise.

The dosser's body must be removed from the pod. How he was to do it he didn't yet know, but it must be taken as far away as possible. And there could be no delay. He must do it that night, or an investigation might lead to its discovery there.

He couldn't think clearly. Father Eustace, the Fallon girl and Bill Peacock had all come to him with questions or information which, when put together, seemed likely to incriminate him. They had only to meet and talk it over for there to be every reason why they should come back to him with even more questions. And yet he wasn't the only resident of the Close who had had contact with the dosser. After all, Phyl Jordan had been the first, when she filled his water bottle. There may have been others. And the dosser's tent had been found in her garden. Everyone had seen it. And it was Bill who had disposed of it. They would find it in his garage.

But who were "they"? The police? Unlikely. They weren't interested. And what would they be investigating? There would be no body. There would be nothing definite to ask. Arlene Fallon had already proved that in her fruitless visit.

No body, and no presumed body. The dosser had simply gone elsewhere, moved on as vagrants do. They were always being moved on, but more often did so of their own accord. End of story.

But he would have to make sure that there really was no body.

He couldn't bring it into the house, or even through the house to put it into the boot of his car, although that was in itself an attractive proposition, since he could drive almost anywhere to get rid of it, somewhere on Otmoor, for example, somewhere quite deserted. But to bring it out to the front of the house was too dangerous, with the front gardens so open to each other. And would it fit in the boot?

Could he handle the body anyway? He thought perhaps he could, with his wheelbarrow. He could get it quite quickly out of his back gate and into the lane. The shape would be awkward to steer on the barrow, but easier if he could wrap it up.

Graham surprised himself with the calm logic of his calculations, since he knew he was in a bit of a state, still trembling from the shock. He thought he deserved another scotch. When he had transferred an amber inch from the bottle and swallowed half of it, he looked around the kitchen. He resented the utter obliviousness of its contents to the feelings he was experiencing. It was just as it had been when he had come back from the hospital after Maddie had died. Furniture, though designed for its purposes (for example, to be leaned on or sat on) showed no eagerness to be so used. The lights had shown no satisfaction at being switched on, nor any relief at being switched off. The gaping slit of the toaster wasn't irritable at being unfilled. The prints on the wall didn't admire themselves. The calendar on the back of the door didn't even know which day it was. The bottle of Dewar's was unaware of its dwindling quantity.

And yet all these things returned his glances with a quiet malevolence that fuelled his feeling of victimisation. "Don't look to us to provide reassurance," they seemed to say. "Ours is the world of normality from which you have been exiled. You don't belong here anymore. You are only here on sufferance."

And it was so, for him. The world accused him of connivance in his own dramas, whether of grief or of guilt. He didn't think he relished his predicament, but he stood outside it, feeling the injustice of it as though it were happening to another person.

Had he been wrong to defend his home against the intrusion of someone who felt that the world owed him a living? It was outrageous that failure should feel aggrieved. There was failure everywhere: failure of government, failure of businesses, failure of individuals. But he wasn't a failure. He had paid his way, always. Why should he suffer? It wasn't his fault that the dosser had invaded his privacy so totally and ruined his opportunity to make money in the process. The dosser wasn't invited. He had been left well alone, but that hadn't been enough. Bambi, she called him? A snowflake. An effete failure. A loser.

How the hours passed he hardly knew. He was transfixed in his chair. He didn't want to think of what was nonetheless lodged in his mind, the maggots in their thousands thrusting each other aside in the blind quest to eat the young man's face, moving in and out of the hair that still remained on the flap of the scalp.

In theory he was hungry, because he hadn't eaten. He even got out the loaf and the butter, but put them away immediately. He couldn't eat, so poured another scotch.

He picked up the newspaper and ran his eye over a column that claimed Jeremy Corbyn was anti-Semitic. He didn't understand these arguments, ever, because he had always thought that Corbyn was himself a Jew. Weren't all these revolutionaries Jewish? Corbyn in his little cap was just like Trotsky. Wasn't Trotsky a Jew? Ann Sims was Jewish, but Graham didn't mind that.

How was he going to deal with the dosser's body? He had decided that he needed to wrap it up, but what could he use? If he had that precious tent, that would have fitted the bill perfectly. It would have kept it all together snug and watertight, and there would have been some justice in putting the dosser back in his tent.

He went upstairs and looked around. Sheets were too thin. He didn't want to feel that he was handling the body directly as far as he could avoid it. He didn't think he was squeamish, but he wanted to distance himself from it as much as he could. It would be possible to roll a body up in a carpet, but there was only the small rug in the hall. Eventually he settled on the slightly quilted bed cover in the spare room. It was usefully thick, but not difficult to roll or fold.

He switched off all the lights downstairs and went up to the bedroom to turn on his bedside lamp. Should anyone be watching the house (why should they?) it ought to appear that everything was normal. His own curtains were drawn. It was very late, but he might be thought to be still reading in bed.

After a while he turned off the lamp, and lay on his bed listening to the sound of almost nothing. He thought he might sleep if he closed his eyes, but realised that his tiredness was accompanied by a tenseness that he didn't think he would ever be rid of. Behind his closed eyes his head thudded. So he opened them again, and grew accustomed to a darkness where all the familiar shapes were faintly defined by the light from a four-way extension socket.

Wouldn't it be wonderful, he thought, if it was all a dream, and he could just drift off and wake later to find himself free of all that he now had to do.

After nearly another hour he felt that he couldn't wait any more. The thing had to be done. He went into the rooms upstairs to look out over the Close in all directions. His neighbours' houses were all dark as far as he could see. The street was still, illuminated by the single street lamp.

He was careful now to use his torch and not put on any lights. He covered the beam with his hands and directed it away from any of the windows. He brought the folded bed cover downstairs, and collected various things from the shed by the back door: a ball of twine, some duct tape and a pair of gardening gloves. These he put in the wheelbarrow that lived propped up against the shed, and set off slowly, with precision, down the path to the pod. He wished he had kept the wheelbarrow better oiled, but the noise wasn't loud enough to be heard, he thought.

The night was still warm, but overcast and muggy. He could see just well enough to avoid a bush and negotiate a step, and didn't need the torch until he got to the pod. There he needed it again briefly to find the keyhole and to see his way inside the pod, again shining it for short moments between his covering fingers, to orientate himself. The flies seemed angered and excited by even this amount of light. He covered most of the torch's beam with a piece of duct tape and laid it on the floor so that the body was just sufficiently illuminated for him to deal with it.

He found it hard to bring himself to touch it. The arm had fallen at an odd angle, as though it were coming apart. He didn't know how far the decomposition extended, how far beneath the clothes the maggots had journeyed, seeking the softer parts, the orifices and membranes most susceptible to collapse, hunching and thrusting, greedy as lovers.

He spread out the bed cover by the body. In the pod it looked almost larger than he needed, and in the fitful gleam of his muffled torch its angular crimson and buff pattern brought back the time that he and Maddie had bought it in Barcelona. Or rather, as always, it was Maddie who had insisted on buying it. What would she say if she could see him now? Something quite true but irritating, he was sure. "You brought this entirely on yourself, Graham." He could hear her rational voice, judging him, regardless of the response she knew it would bring.

He nudged the body over on to the bed cover with his toe, first at the shoulder, then at the hip. The head did an almost 90 degree turn and flopped down with a slight thud. He could see a scattering of maggots that had fallen from it, now isolated on the bed cover, writhing and reaching for some impossible purchase on the flesh they had been shaken from. He moved the body again with his toes, getting it further on to the cover, and then started to roll it up.

He was anxious that it shouldn't lie at its full extent, because the longer it was, the harder it would be to handle on the barrow, but tucking up the legs seemed impossible, and the arms stuck out at odd angles. He did the best he could, and used a lot of duct tape.

Once out of the pod, he found he could do without the torch, but the barrow with its burden was difficult to handle. Bushes and clumps of grasses impeded the way through his neglected gate, and he had occasionally to retreat and then push harder over obstructions. It was easier in the lane, where he decided to turn left. He remembered a path into the fields up there, but wasn't sure if there was a gate or a stile.

It was a stile. Of course. Weren't there sometimes cows in the fields? He remembered now. Cows, and blackberry bushes. The farmer needed protection, but the locals, mindful of rights-of-way, liked their access and their bramble jelly. Graham knew now that he had to get to the river. If the body was found in the river it would solve everything. The dosser would have fallen in after shooting up or inhaling too much coke, or had a fight with a dealer. No one would know who he was, anyway. He would be unrecognizable. And he might drift very far downstream before being found.

Graham had to get the body over the stile. There was no question about it. He brought the wheelbarrow right up to the stile and lugged the body up against the wooden bar. When he had climbed over, he reached back and pulled as hard as he could. The body was lying at an angle across the stile, stiff enough for it to act as a fulcrum, but it was heavy to tilt and pull over. Eventually it slid down and lay across the step on Graham's side.

From there he had to drag it. He did think about getting the barrow over the stile as well, but decided that it was both too heavy and would make too much noise. Was this a mistake? After about thirty yards he began to think so. The unevenness of the ground meant that some of the duct tape was coming undone, and he was just as exhausted as if he had manhandled the barrow over the stile. And what harm would the noise have done at this distance from the houses?

He thought that there might be another hundred yards to go. The path ran beside a hedge of hawthorn and sloe, occasionally suffocated by brambles. Whenever he paused, out of breath, hands on knees, he knew he was doing himself no good. Perhaps there would be a place where he could leave the body beneath the bushes? But having once had the idea of getting it into the river, and therefore as far away from Yarnfield Close as possible, he didn't want to stop now.

What was that noise?

He didn't expect to encounter an animal at this still hour, at least not an animal moving quickly. And towards him. The sound was the sound of rapid legs in the tall dry grasses. Not a muntjac. They were shy, and would keep away. An animal running across the field towards him. He could now hear it panting.

Just as he turned around he realised what it was, and what its presence implied. It was a golden Labrador. It was Father Eustace's dog Effie.

She knew him, of course. And she knew that he was unfriendly. But at this hour of the night? With all its freedom of crannies and smells and unusual creatures in the grass? And with his own distinctive smell that she recognised and was fascinated by? She was a liberated dog, ready to greet Graham effusively and forgive him for everything. She wetly nosed his pungent knees, whimpering and crouching.

Then she investigated the strange large bone-toy that Graham had been playing with and had presumably brought for her to play with too. She tried to turn it over. What was it? It was too large to throw and be retrieved, but its own enticing smell and the fact that Graham was playing with it convinced her that she could play with it too. She had never come across a bone like it, one that was also rather like the lining of her sleeping basket and probably not for burying. But that smell! She became even more excited, running up and down by the side of the body, still more or less wrapped in its Spanish bed cover, nudging it and moaning with delight.

Graham thought that in another ideal existence he might be possessed of a gun with a silencer, and could have shot Effie. As it was, he could think of nothing that he could immediately do. He didn't even contemplate issuing commands. It would be like saying "Go home!" to a force of nature. He looked about him in despair.

There, further back up the path he had taken, not more than forty yards away, with a torch probing the darkness in front of him, stood the expected figure who would put an end to all evasion and concealment: Father Eustace.